SOMETHING LIKE BREATHING

SOMETHING
LIKE BREATHING

Angela Readman

SHEFFIELD – LONDON – NEW YORK

First published in 2019 by And Other Stories
Sheffield – London – New York
www.andotherstories.org

9 8 7 6 5 4 3 2 1

This book is a work of fiction. Any resemblance to actual persons, living or dead, events or places is entirely coincidental.

ISBN: 978-1-911508-30-4
eBook ISBN: 978-1-911508-31-1

Editor: Anna Glendenning; Copy-editor: Fraser Crichton; Proofreader: Sarah Terry; Typesetter: Tetragon, London; Typefaces: Linotype Neue Swift and Verlag; Cover Design: Tree Abraham. Printed and bound by the CPI Group (UK) Ltd, Croydon, CR0 4YY.

A catalogue record for this book is available from the British Library.

This book was supported using public funding by Arts Council England.

PART I

LORRIE

I could tell you about Sylvie, but you wouldn't believe me. I have just one photo. It fluttered out of her dustbin and lodged by our door. It's a blur of a girl stretching her cardigan over a filthy skirt. She has these skinny fawn legs, ready to canter if you looked at her sideways. It's impossible to figure out the look on her face. The girl is a streak, smudging herself out of the camera's gaze. She prefers life that way. Hushed, soft at the edges. I hear that hasn't changed. I haven't seen her in years, though I hear whispers. Girls swearing there's someone looking over their shoulder. They say she'll appear if they fall off their bikes, or fly a kite too close to the cables, and, just as quick as she came, she'll disappear in the mist.

It was windy. The dustbin lid clattered, rolling along the path. I picked up the photo and squirrelled it in my drawer, knowing I'd want it someday. I'm in the picture too: feathers stuck in my hair. I look stunned, mouth open, gormless with confusion. It's not pretty. If you asked Sylvie about the feathers, she'd say she doesn't remember. She'd change the subject to wild flowers, puffins, or something, anything, other than her. So, it's me who's going to tell you about Sylvie. Like it or not, someone must.

I was all about rabbits; she was all about chickens. Looking out the window I saw whiskers, cottontails hopping all over, making the poppies quiver. The girl next door stood beside a chicken. Now I saw her, now I didn't. The apple tree shuffled in the breeze and covered the girl with leaves. When the wind settled, and I had a clear view, she was gone.

My mother and father stood outside staring up, brows crinkled, knotting their thoughts into one.

'It's so dark in Lorrie's room,' Mum said. 'We should cut that tree down. It's crazy.'

The saw dangled in my father's hands. He circled the trunk, looking. 'It's so close to the cottage, though. Cut it wrong and we could lose the roof.'

Mum wandered to the back door and glanced back, laying a hand on her collarbone.

'I wonder how deep the roots go.'

Roots were a problem. She could almost feel them writhing under the house and pulling us all underground.

'That tree's fine,' Grumps said at dinner. 'It's a rare thing on this side of the island. The story goes my grandmother brought over a seed and planted it herself.'

'I know,' my mother said. 'It's a lovely tree, but it's so near the house.'

'If we want to cut it down, we'll have to get someone in,' my father said. 'Just to be on the safe side.'

Grumps rolled his eyes. We could almost see him add *Cut down a tree* to his mental list of things his son-in-law couldn't do. Mum rose from the table carrying plates.

'It can wait.'

That was that, for now the tree stayed. They were picking their battles, considering the lead water pipes and the woodworm in the kitchen cupboards. She pulled a pencil from behind Toby's ear and scribbled *Do Something about that Tree* on her list.

'Every time I tick something off I add seven things,' she said.

'You're that Greek fella.' There was a lake of gravy next to Toby's hillside of potato. He mushed it into a landslide without mercy.

'What?' She tilted her head. I've seen dogs with their head at the same angle waiting for their owner to return. My mother was fascinated by my brother. He dangled morsels of conversation for her and she leapt for the snippets, shiny as liver. He told her about some bloke pushing a boulder uphill every day, only to start over at sunrise. She rose from the table and said, 'Yup, me and him should have a cuppa sometime. We may be soulmates.' I never heard her use that word any other time.

The water coughed into the sink loud as an old man catching a lungful of the morning.

'The water looks cloudy again.' Mum pushed back her hair with soapy fingers, suds fizzing in her ear. 'I suppose I should call the plumber.'

The days of saying the place needed 'a little tender loving care' were over, though that's how she had pitched it before we came here. It was a solid cottage, she said, a beautiful place to grow up. It could be lovely with a lick of paint. We were going. That was that. Grumps slipped a disc shifting a barrel and our whole life was folded into crates and driven north.

The horizon opened as we left the city. The land folded around us. The clouds laid their shadows on the hills. Mario Lanza crooned out the window to a shiver of lavender and started to hiss. He gave up, resigned to the radio losing a signal. The static was as loud as the rain.

We boarded the ferry quietly, bored of I spy featuring mostly mountains and lakes. I clung to the railing, face streaming, tears pinched out by the wind. I stared at the mainland we were leaving behind. The life I'd known narrowed to a streak. The sea heaved. The keel kept us all gripping the railings, except for my father. When the rain cleared, and my mother insisted we huddle together to have our picture taken on the deck, he held the camera and let himself rock with the boat.

It was funny, how he never put up much of a fight about moving. He had to give up his job selling insurance, and he hated Cullen skink. He couldn't stand mackerel, or weather. Or wildlife, or chit-chat. In short, he cared for the island about as much as he cared for his father-in-law, who, on a good day, he called the Mule-Headed Man. Toby and I called him Grumps. It had been a secret when we were little, but when we blurted it out in front of him one Christmas the old man laughed and we saw no need to stop. Grumps was who he was, he was proud of it, and glad we'd found out. There was no need for pointless small talk any more. He could finally break wind in public. He could see a neighbour approaching, mutter 'fuck that', and we wouldn't judge.

We drove towards the distillery, the roads winding, steam rising from the chimneys and fusing with the clouds. The small windows were coppery, glinting in the sun. We drove on to the cottage. Our belongings all arrived long before we did. Every stick of furniture we owned was sitting outside on the grass. Grumps stood in the middle of it shaking his head.

'You've got a tonne of stuff.' He squinted along the lane, waiting for another van to show up and dump the world on his back. The man was a distiller. The idea of a flawed batch was never far away. Even at his happiest, he never lost that look that something could happen and pour it all down the drain at any time.

'You're looking well.' Dad lit a cigarette and looked for an ashtray, briefly forgetting the lounge he was standing in was outside. Toby and I glared at our mother. If Grumps was well, couldn't she stop worrying about him rattling around the place all by himself? Couldn't we all hop in the car and turn around? The distillery was open. It was business as usual, even if its owner used a cane on damp days, had stopped ironing his shirts and ate cereal for every meal. Mum pointed at the creases on his shirt and frowned.

'It's not like I'm trying to impress anyone.' Grumps smoothed out his pocket. 'Who's going be offended by a wrinkle or two? Why cook? Who can make anything better than cornflakes anyhow?'

'Can I have cereal for dinner?' Toby asked.

There was a chorus of 'No'. Mum started it. I was glad to prolong it.

Those first weeks were spent swooping through the cottage clearing the cupboards. My mother forever had a cloth in her hand. There were cobwebs in the pantry, wasps in the sugar and mouse droppings on the floor. The distillery was clean as a pin, but the cottage was irrelevant for a man on his own. It was a place to eat, sleep, dress for work, and do it all again the next day, and the next. Grumps didn't mind spiders or cobwebs. Without his glasses, he no longer noticed the silverfish. The carpet in my room writhed, a tide of spines under my feet. I got so used to the sheen I told my parents it could stay. They rolled up my opinion and carried the carpet downstairs anyway.

I festered in my bedroom, a fortress of boxes. Toys, Books, Clothes and Bits and Bobs. The sound of the wind in the leaves outside resembled traffic, if I closed my eyes. I could imagine strolling along the street we used to live on in England. The paint on the door of our house was purple. Next door's was yellow. The buildings of the terrace were identical, but each house found a way to be itself.

On fine days, my mother wouldn't always make me go to school. 'You'll catch up tomorrow,' she'd say, 'it's the first day of summer. Time to learn the feeling of the sun on your face.' We'd wander to the park, ignoring the 'Keep Off the Grass' signs. We used to sit on our coats and tuck into our lunch in waxy bags from the bakery. It wasn't possible to walk past without salivating. The aroma of sweet buns glazed with honey would waft onto the street and we'd breathe deep. The bakery was so close to our house we bought something several times a week. Then we didn't. My mother would cross the street to buy bread from the burnt-bottom place instead. My father wouldn't look the baker in the eye. I'd see him turn over his bread, inspect his slice of disappointment and sigh. 'I'm not sure I put that cigarette out properly,' he'd say, scurrying to his office to check the ashtrays.

Eventually, we stopped eating bread altogether. Mum did without her lemon curd on toast, rather than risk inspiring another conversation about insurance, and the importance of planning your escape routes in advance of an emergency. There was only one spare set of sheets in the linen cupboard on the day we moved out. My father had taken the rest and knotted them into ladders we could dangle out the window of the top floor.

I pushed my hands over my ears to block out the shuffle of the wind in the leaves. I hated the island. I hated the sulky skies and the rustling quiet. I swore I'd never unpack. If I did, it would be saying: This is it, this is my life. I'll never leave.

THE DIARY OF . . . SYLVIE TYLER.
KEEP OUT!
(I MEAN IT, MA)

The lass bursts out of the Ford like it can't contain her. *Pow!* The parents and the wee lad follow, his ears are peachy-coloured cups lit up by the sun. I'm looking out. The mother's stretching all over like a cat in pedal pushers. She's wandering about inspecting this and that, polishing the china cabinet with a hankie. Everyone's picking up lamps and pointing to scuffs on the dresser. They all look dead amazed anything's still in one piece. That is, everyone but the lass.

She drags a pouf to a chair, brushes a bee off a sunflower-patterned cushion and sits. Arms folded. Firm. I freeze behind the curtains like she's mummified me or something. I can't budge, and I can't look at anything but her. I reckon she'll never go inside and might just live outside in the wild for all her days like a hare. Just because she can.

Everyone's carting stuff indoors, except for her. She's slipping pink sunglasses off the top of her head and staring at the clouds. The sky is her cinema. I picture doing the same, just sitting, thumbs twiddling, while everyone else is skittering about. I could never do that. I'd have to carry stuff in. I'd be in the kitchen already, knee-deep in newspaper. I'd be listening to Ma give me a sermon on how to correctly stack the bowls.

The lass is bonnie, feisty looking, and bored. I bet she'd rather be blowing bubbles into orange juice with a straw. Or hanging cocktail-stick fangs out of her gob, just because folk say it's rude. She looks up and I lurch from the window, heart filling like a balloon. *Pop!* It could burst. It's aching to know her that much.

Urgh, I doubt that sort of lassie would knock around with me anyway. And if she did, what good would it do? Ma would hate it. 'What do you need friends for? I'm your friend,' she's always saying, 'I'm the only friend you have or need.' This has to be the saddest sentence any lassie my age ever wrote, I know.

LORRIE

I rushed to the garden and she was gone. The same as yesterday, and the day before. The shape of her sandals lay on the grass, and a trail of dropped corn was leading to her door. She'd caught the sound of the key in the lock, heard me coming and run. The rabbits nibbled the spot where she'd stood, pulling her long socks up over her knees.

I never saw her stroke the rabbits. She only had eyes for chickens. The fluffy white one was her favourite. On Saturday morning, it strutted beside her, a feathery shadow to every step she took. The girl put a hand into her bag of feed and waited. I raced out in my slippers. This time, she wouldn't hear me coming. She was mine.

'What you doing?' I poked my nose through the fence. I'd assumed she was the same age as me, but now I looked closely, I figured she must be younger, even though she was taller. She wore a violet ribbon in plaits the colour of barley and her cardigan had those tiny pearly buttons mothers sew on jackets for babies. She looked at me and reminded me of a child peering out from her mother's skirts. The paper bag rustled in her hand. The chicken paused. She dropped some corn and took a step backwards. The bird's feet clawed the dirt. It followed her without turning around.

'You're teaching the chicken to walk backwards? Brilliant!' I said. 'I'm Lorrie.'

I'd scraped my wrist poking a hand through the fence. The girl didn't shake it. There wasn't a hostility to her, not exactly. I'd think about it later and decide it was more that she was considering whether to smile and was undecided. I wondered if she was deaf, or if the cat had got her tongue. Grumps sometimes kept the company of a cat that hung around the distillery. It was a wild thing with a patch missing from one ear, a scar on its flank, and the stare of a boxer with a famous fight under his belt. That cat probably could catch someone's tongue. I wouldn't be surprised. I wouldn't be surprised at anything here. Everything was so still, and quivering at the same time. The wind switched and the grass darkened, shivering with creatures looking for somewhere to curl up and die.

Not long after we arrived, I found an owl on the doorstep. Stone cold, out of nowhere. 'Is it dead? How did that happen?' Grumps winced at my shrieks and grabbed the dustpan without saying a word. That was his style. Silence was the style of everyone on the island, as en vogue as chunky socks and wellies. Here, it wasn't always possible to avoid someone who annoyed you. Instead of confrontation people made their faces stone walls.

Even my mother was quieter than she was before we came. It seemed she'd found part of herself she'd left in her old room with pictures of tightrope walkers on the wall. She no longer ever said, out of nowhere, 'I fancy doing something, let's go to a matinee.' There was nowhere to go. Instead, she fostered long silences and staring out at the peeling paint on the gate and the boot prints the workmen left in the lane. I found the quiet so disturbing I did anything to avoid it.

I started following my grandfather to the distillery most afternoons. If I stayed in and admitted I was bored, my mother would reel off a list of chores I could do: peel wallpaper, dust, or unpack. I polished copper pipes with my sleeve and listened to Grumps evaluate whisky instead. He swirled a sparkling glass and held it to the light, nose perched over the liquid, sharp as a park-keeper at his pond.

'Nose: a vanilla scent with a hint of smoke.' He took a sip. 'Palate: Toffee with an undertone of . . . ' He paused, considering his words, more words than I'd ever heard him say in one go. The drink all looked the same to me, but I couldn't stop listening. This was his poetry. He spoke the language of whisky with absolute certainty. Here, I caught a glimpse of where he really lived.

AN EVALUATION OF MY GRANDFATHER

Nose: Ginger beer, grain, the sugar he puts in the wasp traps. A residue of whisky lingers on his clothes. It runs through his veins. He carries the aroma of the roast chicken he peels into strips at lunchtime and places in a bowl by the distillery for the cat without a collar. He watches it eat the breast while he chomps the skin. No matter how close the cat gets, he never strokes it. Never even tries. It carries the scent of small bloody deaths, but he doesn't mind. He enjoys the honesty of its hostile company more than a pet he could hold in his hands.

Palate: Whisky, crackers he dips into jars of chutney and pickled onions. He smacks the juice out of the lines around his lips with a slurping sound and never laughs off his lack of manners. Smiles are not something he scatters. When he does crack a smile, it has the power to make my mother recall suppers she had growing up when her parents didn't really say much, but knew what the other was thinking because it was what they were thinking themselves.

Finish: He wears whatever hangs on the hook of his door, shirts and trousers that never match. For his whole life, someone got out his clothes for him. First his mother, then his wife, would iron what he should wear for the day and lay it flat on the bed. He makes little effort to learn what clothes might sit right together, even when my mother tries to give him pointers. He continues wearing chequered patterns with spots, red with green, any mismatched clothes he stumbles across. He's as steadfast to clashing colours as a man is to a uniform. It is a uniform, a uniform of grief serving the memory of his late wife.

Overall: A man who brings a thimbleful of whisky and honey when I have a cold. He'll tell me a story, but only if I ask for it to be told. It's the same story each time. For a few minutes, he tells it and I see someone other than my grandfather – I just see a man, who was once a boy, who once fell for a surly girl.

Grumps shooed me out of the distillery, sick of me following him around. I put on my roller skates and jolted around the gritty lane, missing the smooth paving of the city. I hadn't seen another kid since we moved in, other than Toby. He'd recently made the decision he wanted to be a magician and I was getting sick of him asking if he could saw me in half. The girl was a lifesaver. I spotted her and wondered if her rabbits could do tricks too. Perhaps something involving hurdles made of sticks and toilet paper. Rabbits racing, hopping over a ribbon staked in the grass. I'd place my bet on the spotted one that was humping her shoes.

'We just moved here,' I said. 'My parents, me and my brother. Grandma died last year. Grumps is getting rickety, so we came. There's a smell in my room of something dead,' I chattered.

She stepped back. Conversation could be contagious. I wanted it to be.

I don't know why I told her about the strange smell in my room, I hadn't got around to complaining to my parents about it yet. I could imagine my mother shaking her head. 'Lorrie,' she'd say, 'I'm sick of your attitude. We're all trying to adjust to life here.' I decided to say nothing to anyone, but it all spilled out anyway. There was something about the girl. I couldn't help it with her. Now I'd told her my life story, I felt a bit better.

'What's your name?' I asked.

A woman with strappy shoes trotted out of the house carrying a large box to her car. 'Sylvie,' she called. 'Come on, we've got appointments. I have to make a sale. Don't dawdle now. We haven't got all day.'

The girl skulked towards her mother, who was jangling her keys, a lucky rabbit's foot dangling off her key ring, pawing the air.

'Sylvie? Is that your name?' I called.

The girl span around, gave a small nod and ran. I waved. I had her name. It was a start.

The lass is here. And she ain't going anywhere. If Ma could wave a sparkly wand or a feather duster and make her disappear she'd do it in a jiffy. *Puff!* But she can't. It makes her do that wee frown. The one that, as soon as she realises she's doing it, forces her to grab a pot of cold cream. Quick.

'That lassie next door's out there again,' I say, 'looking for us.'

Lorrie's poking a sandal through the fence. Ma looks out the window, 'If you ignore her, she'll go away,' she's saying.

So I try to, all week, I ignore her like a whiffer in church. I keep my head down when I'm feeding the chickens, feart to look up in case the lassie meets my eye. And still she keeps wandering over, yattering my ear off. There's this painter who did sunflowers and cut his ear off once. I reckon that's what happened to him.

'I dunno how long I can ignore her for, Ma. Won't it look weird if I do?'

If there's one thing I shouldn't look, it's weird. If Ma could knit me a gansey to match the wallpaper, she would, I reckon. Lassies like me should blend in. Be good. Be sweet. Be as ordinary as we can.

'Hmm, I suppose it won't hurt to be polite,' she says. 'Just don't be too friendly to her.'

I know what 'too friendly' means. I found out when I was four and she banned me from speaking to that wee lad in callipers EVER AGAIN. Do you hear me? Sylvie, NEVER. I MEAN IT. I haven't been too friendly since. I keep my gob shut, in company anyhow. Women blether and I stare at the buckles on my shoes. Kids blabber and I'll think of something dead interesting to say, but the words clag in my throat before I can spit anything out. It makes school this never-ending spelling test full of words you could spell yesterday, but can't picture once you're holding the pen. Lorrie never notices. That's why she's fantastic. She's so busy havering, I never have to worry about being struck dumb. I tell Ma this and she hmms, slathering a greeny face mask all over her cheeks like the witch in *The Wizard of Oz*. Maybe that's what was wrong with her, she was just scared of the wrinkles setting in.

'The child does have excellent posture, I'll give her that. Hmm. You could invite her over. Just don't – '

'I know, I know,' I say. There's no need for her to finish. I know the rules. Don't say much about myself, keep my mouth shut, and for heaven's sake, Sylvie . . .

I put on my nightie and peek out before bed. I listen to the pip of a bird and stare at the light over the fence. That's her room, Lorrie, my pal. Maybe. If she looks out she'll see me. Lorrie and Sylvie. Sylvie and Lorrie, waving across the way. Flicking the lights on and off, knocking about. Ordinary lasses. Just like everyone else.

LORRIE

Bunny Tyler believed in God and Tupperware. I'm not sure which she believed in more. Wherever she went, she carried a duck-egg handbag containing a Bible, a revolutionary cheese grater, and a storage pot. One hand remained on the clasp, ready to whip out the contents at any given moment, should anyone need spiritual guidance. There was no Tupperware on the island until she discovered it; even the mainland had never set eyes on it before.

Bunny's pen pal in Florida had sent her a sample. Caroline Craig was married to a man Bunny's husband served with. The wives, both lonely and curious about life beyond their front doors, started corresponding at the suggestion of their husbands.

I buried my sister today, Caroline wrote. *We hadn't seen each other for years. I drove across two states with a truck full of Bundt cake. Bringing something was the only thing that stopped me going crazy. When I got there, the cake was still fresh as a daisy. Thank God for Tupperware!*

It hadn't been long since Bunny's husband suddenly passed away. In the time it takes letters to cross in the post, everything had changed. Bunny picked up a pen and found herself unable to write the words 'my husband has died'. Instead, she'd replied asking her friend to tell her more about this Tupperware, please.

It was shiny and clean. It made everything last so much longer. Bunny imported a crate and set about converting the island with a missionary zeal.

'This will change your life!' she said, whipping out a salad pot in the grocers. Women in the village still quoted the occasion. It was proof she has airs and graces, that one, always has, always will.

It wasn't only storage pots that took Bunny's fancy. Whenever the mood struck her, she'd import a box full of some kitchen gadget or other, and set out to sell it to whoever she met. 'You wouldn't believe what I have to show you! This will save you so much time . . . ' she'd say, waving around a peeler that made short work of potatoes. 'I can save hours of your life. Just look!'

I skipped around to Sylvie's and avoided the hinges on the gate, sticky with oil. There were no men living at the property, not that I knew of, but a man arrived every weekend, always carrying something. Last week, he brought an oilcan.

The rabbits dusted my shoes with their tails. I bent down.

'Can I pick one up?' I cradled a rabbit and rubbed the sunlight in its ears. 'What's his name?'

'Pie.' Sylvie studied the grass on her shoes.

'What's *his* name?' I pointed at a rabbit so perfect my brother would have done anything to pull it out of a hat.

'Stew.'

I didn't understand. Not straight away. The rabbits weren't christened because they weren't pets. Their job was to breed and hop into pans, their leftovers interned in plastic coffins in the cold store. Bunny was saving for a fridge. She dreamed of drinking milk in the middle of the night without trudging outside in her dressing gown. If I'd known about the rabbits, I'm not sure I'd have waved at her carrying an armful of kitchenware and trotting across the lawn in her heels.

'You must be from next door? Lorrie, is it? Lovely to meet you.'

The sunlight was a halo behind her, cupping her curls. Bunny beamed as if angels or the King of Kitchen Gadgets had landed on her lawn.

'I'm so sorry about your grandmother last year. Lovely lady,' she said. 'I'd let her have my redcurrants and she'd give me her apples, so we could both make jelly all year round. Well, she's gone to a better place now.'

The plastic boxes in her arms slotted into one another Russian-doll style. Bunny looked down at them as she said 'better place' and I couldn't be sure if she meant my grandmother had gone to heaven or Tupperwareland.

'Come on in,' she said. 'I'll make lemonade.'

Bunny charged around her kitchen sprinkling sugar and slicing lemons. It was nothing to whip up a batch. When it came to Bunny Tyler and I, everything was nothing. If I came over after supper, apple crumble withheld because I'd grabbed a crowbar and lifted the floor in my room, she'd whip out the caramel wafers, or pop open a container of lavender shortbread. No problem. Nothing was too much trouble, providing I followed her rules: cross my legs at the ankles, use a coaster and always say please and thank you.

'It's wonderful to see Sylvie with such a confident girl. Perhaps you could teach her a thing or two.'

Bunny proffered the biscuit barrel, looking at her daughter. I'd once seen a beauty queen hand over her crown with the same look on her face. Beautiful disappointment.

'If you'd only speak up and smile now and then, like Lorrie,' she said, 'people might like you!'

'I like her as she is,' I said.

I wasn't sure if I did yet. Sylvie was so quiet I wasn't sure there was much to like, but in the conspiracy of children against adults it was the right thing to say. Bunny stirred clanking ice in the frosty jug. Sylvie scratched her knuckles, back and forth, in the same place until the skin was raw. I sensed a silent war between them I was fighting both sides of. I was a hero and a traitor all at the same time.

The kitchen was lemon. The plastic table was cleaner than ice.

'It's a lovely room,' I said. 'My mother would be so jealous.'

Don't ask me how I knew this was the right thing to say to get in Bunny's good books, but I did. Bunny dreamed of owning more kitchen gadgets than any other woman on the island, and displaying them with the most flair. I knew it, even then, I knew her kind. It wasn't so different to mine.

'I just had it painted. I had that dresser built to fit there.' Bunny pointed at the dresser.

The wood was painted fire-engine red. Whoever made her it had sawed a heart and the silhouettes of a pair of rabbits into the plinth.

The room was the same as ours, but in reverse. The window was on the opposite side. The hob sparkled. I could see what my parents meant when they stared at crumbling walls and said, 'I can see the potential.' This was a life they could see, if everything was put away and labelled correctly, which it wasn't.

We'd been spooning sugar out of the coffee canister since I'd found the rat under my floor. I'd been desperate to get to the bottom of the smell in my room. The crowbar was lying on the stairs, carpet fibres still clinging to the steel. I pried up one floorboard, then another, and brought the rat down by the tail. Dangling. Its skeleton visible, poking out of the fur. I winced to hold it, but I wanted my mother to see. I wanted her to realise I'd lifted a floorboard under the bed she'd slept in as a girl. It wasn't the only thing I'd found.

'Do you want the tour?'

Bunny led us to the lounge. The plastic-covered sofa broke wind when Sylvie flopped down, but Bunny didn't giggle. She stood by the TV the way a salesman stands beside a new car. No one on the island had ever owned a television before Bunny Tyler, she wanted me to know.

'It was the craziest thing. I got it with the life insurance. Women kept calling around the week it arrived. Their kids pressed their snotty noses against the window, smearing the glass to get a peek!' she said. 'You're welcome over anytime, Lorrie, if there's anything you want to see.'

I suddenly loved her. There was no set at home yet. Dad always promised to get one as soon as he got a bonus. But no matter how many life insurance policies he sold, he always fell short. It wasn't that he was a lousy salesman, as such. If anything, he painted a picture of disaster too well. People couldn't wait to shoo him out of the house. They had some-where to go. Someone to meet, dinner was ready. His *what would happen if . . .* was enough to put anyone off their shep-herd's pie.

There was a faded Virgin Mary figure on Bunny's fireplace. The afternoon sun streamed through the curtains and bleached her features a little more each day. The statue's painted lips were almost as pale as her face. Bunny wasn't a Catholic, but she'd had the figure since childhood. Whenever she went out, she patted it and said, 'Look after the house.' Whenever she came in, she ignored it. Next to Mary, a pair of wrinkled boots stood on the shelf. It appeared they'd been walking through mud and frozen with their laces undone.

'The sun's coming out anyway. That reminds me, I've left plastic in the car.' Bunny flitted out to save her storage pots from warped lids. I nudged Sylvie in the ribs.

'What's with the boots?'

'They're his,' Sylvie said. 'They're the Miracle Boots.'

I had to hold my breath when she spoke. Really listen. If I missed a word, she'd never repeat it. The way she breathed *his* made me think Jesus had stopped by, slipped his sandals off at the door and come in for a cuppa without leaving a footprint on Bunny's freshly scrubbed carpet.

'What do you mean?' I asked, but Sylvie was off, trudging upstairs to her room.

I followed. Beyond the swallows on the walls and the canary in a cage by the window, I could see my bedroom window. It looked cleaner at a distance.

'Have you been sick?' I gestured to a jug of flowers, a pot of vapour rub and a packet of cough drops by the bed.

'Not lately,' Sylvie said. 'I'm always poorly though.'

'Always?'

'Pretty much.'

The canary started to sing. Its throat was a yellow pulse bobbing in and out, brighter than a summer's afternoon. Sylvie kicked a glossy stack of magazines under the bed and slammed a diary in the drawer, flustered.

'You've got more than one copy of the same book.' I pointed to a shelf higgledy-piggledy with books for identifying birds and wild flowers, plus several editions of *Alice's Adventures in Wonderland*.

'I love comparing the illustrations. Look.'

Sylvie turned to a page bookmarked by a folded Tunnock's wrapper.

'This Alice is beautiful, but that one looks wise, like a little old woman is locked inside her somewhere.'

The page didn't interest me as much as annuals about girls solving crimes of stolen peppermints at school, or my mother's film magazines, but I looked. Sylvie had never showed me anything before. Every word from her had to be dragged out slower than pulling a splinter. She made it look as painful.

'Look at this one, compared to this.'

She flicked through the pages, showing me her favourite illustrations. If I was dying to hear about the Miracle Boots? Tough. I'd have to wait. I'd never seen her look so enthusiastic about anything.

So, I'm standing there with Lorrie. And everyone's giggling. And trying to be clever. And making me look stupid. That's school all over, I reckon. It's just there to make some folk look clever. And Lorrie can see it. She's wearing this cardigan the colour of wild hyacinths and her hair's all shiny ripples like a breeze on a loch. The kids are all clutching their lunchboxes and peering at her behind fringes cut with kitchen scissors. Hands twitching at their sides, desperate to stroke a shiny new pet. *Oow. Who's that girl? Where's she from? I heard the mainland. I heard she lives at the distillery. She looks like someone from a city. You can tell.*

They're all buzzing around. Buzz. Buzz. Buzz. I gaze at the ground like it's a night sky with one star. There's a tooth on the pavement someone must have lost without noticing it fall. Milk white on the concrete. Some lassie kicks it along the hopscotch, coming over to ask Lorrie if she puts in plaits before bed. To ask where she lives. Who her brother is.

'That weeny kid with the tousie hair? The one with the lugs?'

'That's him . . . I like your ponytail,' Lorrie says. 'I like your skirt.'

She likes everything about everyone. I can tell she's smiling even without looking. I keep staring at the tooth, wondering if some wean somewhere is bawling to his mammy he missed his chance to make a mint off the tooth fairy. I won't look up. I can't. The lasses are all giggling at the pinafore Ma made me wear. Some are making that goldfish face at me. I hear their lips smackety smacking and wonder if Lorrie's still smiling. I bet she is.

'Why do they make that fishy face at you?' she says once they're gone.

I open my gob and nowt comes out. It slaps shut like haddock. The kids are all wandering across the playground, back to jumping elastics and juggling balls against the wall. Lorrie shuffles towards the skipping ropes.

'You want to join in?' she's asking. 'Over there.'

I peek up at the lasses who laugh at me as they twirl both ends. Skipping so fast my feet feel like hooves. I'm dead slow compared to other folks, I reckon. I'm too scared I'll fall and rip my dress. Ma would wallap me for getting clatty.

'Do you mind if I . . . ?'

Lorrie hops off to join the skippers. I watch her jump and not fall, jump and not fall, until Miss comes out and shakes the brass bell to herd us into class.

LORRIE

The school was a squat building surrounded by a stone wall. To get there, it was impossible not to pass the harbour. Lobster pots piled high, glimpses of fishing boats rocking in the wind. Even the teachers stared out the window most afternoons, aware of the sea so close by, locked outside. There was only one school on the island. The children came from all sides. A few from the north side streamed off a small bus, but most walked. It was one of the first things I noticed about people who were born on the island. The girls all had calves stocky as June lambs, sturdy from walking uphill. Even the smallest girls looked solid and wary, ducking away from their mothers' kisses and instructions to behave. They were all curious about me. Or, rather, where I'd been, what I'd seen. They saw me as a walking encyclopaedia of distant lands. Only a few had ever left the island, in their fathers' vans packed with supplies, or gripping the hands of their mothers on the way to pick up spectacles or dentures from the mainland. They saw the smoky outlines of factories and were ushered onto the ferry, venturing no further into the city than necessary.

The kids all shuffled towards me now, posing questions about massive roller coasters, zoos, department stores as big as cathedrals, toy shops with life-sized bears in the windows and train sets that ran around and around on tracks above their heads.

'Is it true there are shops that sell nothing but wedding dresses?' a girl called Marjorie asked. 'I heard there were thousands of them all in a row, all different shades of white.'

'Don't be daft. How can there be more than one shade of white? White's white,' someone said.

I reassured Marjorie, yes it was true. There were bridal shops with dresses as different as snowflakes, sparkling, plain, high-necked or low, in lace, or in cotton. In cities, there were more shades of white than the island had seen winters, anything was possible. I stretched the truth and made everything bigger, and brighter, and louder, and faster than it was, but I loved being an expert on something. It gave me a glamour that faded as soon I traipsed back into the classroom with Sylvie.

Miss Jones chalked a lily on the blackboard and pointed out each part.

'Does anyone know what this is called?'

The wooden ruler dipped from leaves to petals and settled on a long strand reaching out of the flower. The class nibbled their pencils, inspecting their teeth marks in the wood. I glanced at Sylvie writing S t a m e n on her page in spidery letters.

'Sylvie?' Miss Jones softened her voice and looked hopeful.

Sylvie opened her mouth, closed it and shook her head.

'Goldfish!' The children giggled.

I glanced at Sylvie's page and my hand shot into the air. 'Stamen,' I said.

If she was angry I stole her answer, I didn't care. People loved me. It was a giddy feeling. I could make anyone adore me without trying. I'm still that way. I'm not being vain, they just do. I have the sort of manners that put smiles on faces I'm not even sure I like.

AN EVALUATION OF SYLVIE TYLER

Nose: There's a scent of wood shavings on her fingers. It's from the pencils she insists on sharpening before they get the chance to snap, and closer still, there's a damp sort of smell that reminds me of coming in from the rain. If you sat close to her, you could smell the strand of hair she swirls and swirls, running it across her lips and sucking it all day.

Palate: The cucumber in the sandwiches her mother packs in tight plastic boxes, caramel wafers with shiny Tunnock's wrappers she always saves, and milk that warms in her satchel. The plastic boxes pop when she opens her lunch, breathy as the gobstopper-scented laughter of kids walking past. I only ever saw Sylvie look disgusted once. It was seeing a boy take a lollipop out of his mouth and giving a lick to a friend. 'I'd never do that,' she'd said. 'I wouldn't dare. Just seeing it makes me feel sick.'

Finish: Pale as the lighthouse, skinny, with a voice that shuffles up to her mouth, if she speaks at all. She folds her shoulders inwards, wearing a sweater that would prefer to be on the shelf. She knows how many floor tiles are between her desk and the blackboard. Or she should do, she looks down often enough. I asked once, as a joke, how many tiles there were. 'Twenty-six,' Sylvie replied, 'and eighteen to the door.'

Overall: This isn't someone I can see myself with, if I'm honest. There are other girls who are more fun. I wander around with Sylvie without allowing myself to look as if I want to, determined not to catch her unpopularity and let it seep in.

The stone bounced along the lane. Sylvie kicked it and let it roll wherever it wanted. The distillery churned steam into the clouds as we passed it. I finally let out what I'd wanted to say all day.

'Why didn't you answer that question in class?' I asked. 'You had the answer.'

The words drifted over us without seeming to touch Sylvie. For a long time, she didn't reply. When she did, it was a whisper.

'I wanted to' – she scratched her knuckles – 'but I couldn't, couldn't get the words out. It happens sometimes, it happens with loads of people . . . except you.'

The slightest smile from Sylvie was a fluffy elephant at the fair. It had to be won with a clear aim, it wasn't given away. I'd won her trust without knowing what I was winning, and not unlike that fluffy elephant I'd once won throwing balls at a coconut stall, now it was mine I wasn't sure I wanted it.

One false move and squish. *Bam!* Ma claps her hands around the moth and lets it out in a jar. I'm watching it flutter fast as my heart, battering against the glass. Ma lifts the suitcase off the wardrobe and cracks on with folding my clothes. The black cardigan. The grey skirt. The dress the colour of a sack of tatties. The jumper with the sleeves that make my arms feel like Frankenstein. It's no wonder he went a bit doolally. The fella that made him could have at least knitted him a sweater that fit.

'I don't want to go,' I say. 'Please, Ma.'

'Don't be daft.' She's balling socks and stuffing a pair into my shoes. 'We always visit your Nan at this time of year. It's lovely to have a change of scenery. She'll be so pleased to see you, you know that.'

I do. And I know I'll be off school for a week. Anything can happen in a week, a week's a lifetime. I'll miss people falling off the swings and skinning their knees, class projects, fights, bogies getting flicked. And sides being taken. And some kids falling out, and others deciding to be pals for life. That's what worries me.

Lorrie gets this look after playtime like Irn-Bru losing its fizz. She breaks away from the other lassies, pulls out her chair from the desk and makes a face worse than nails on a blackboard, like it hurts to sit near me. If she could, she'd be somewhere else. Off and away with Robin Macleod and the cattle her folks

37

keep. I don't blame her. I'd be like Robin myself, if I could. Loud. Funny. Bonnie. If I could get the words out, anyhow. The jokes I want to tell always sit on my tongue for so long someone else always gets them out first. I'm forever practising everything in my head. Just to make sure it doesn't sound wrong.

'I can't go anywhere,' I say to Ma. 'If I do, when I come back Lorrie and Robin will be pals and I'll be left out.'

'You can all be friends together. If being away for a week makes someone forget you, you don't want them to be your friend.'

She doesn't get it. The lassies at school don't flit around in flocks. They flutter into pairs like giggly lovebirds practising mating for life. I keep trying to explain, but it comes out all wrong. If lassies were the same when Ma was my age, she's forced herself to forget. I reckon it's the only way mas can be mas.

My nightie flaps into the suitcase soft as a bird giving up flight.

'Don't make something out of nothing!' Ma says.

I've got a face like a slapped arse and I know it, if the wind changes I'll stay this way forever. 'It's not the end of the world. It's just one weekend.'

It's never just a weekend. And she knows it.

Slam! The case snaps shut. The blouse hanging out of the side looks a bit like I feel. Trapped. I'm dying to say: Ma, I wish you'd listen. I hate Nan's house. It reeks. I hate the pong of fusty lavender and mouldy bread. The pinch of her Baltic fingers clawing for a cuddle, wrinkled mouth puckering up for a peck. I can't stand her cigarettes, all that smoke and ghosts swirling around her. Everyone she talks about is dead. I can't stand her. I can't say that though. Ma would wash my mouth out with soap like the day I kissed that boy in the wee park with the swings.

The case stands by the standard lamp like a signpost saying: *You'll do what I tell you to do. You don't get a say.*

Ma picks up the jar with the moth and carries it out. I listen to her open the back door and release it. The door creaks. The moth flies free for a minute, before I hear it battering at the window something rotten. It beats itself senseless trying to get in again.

LORRIE

Bunny had a diamond on her finger and no need to chop her own firewood. Seth Johnson had proposed on a Sunday. Everyone was looking. Outside the church, a cluster of rust- and mustard-coloured hats twisted to face the couple, slow as sunflowers searching for the sun. Seth got on one knee, crushing fallen leaves on the ground.

'I wanted to do this now, not on a workday. This doesn't feel like work. Mrs Tyler, will you marry me?'

It was strange to see him address her as Mrs Tyler when we saw him at her place so often. Every week, he would wander up Bunny's path carrying a toolbox, a few bottles of beer, and something for the lady of the house: a cabbage, a jar of honey, a coat rack, a pot of varnish for her fence. He always knocked once, then strolled right in. I could only put it down to everyone watching: Mrs Tyler sounded more suitable for an audience. The congregation grinned, some were already clapping. Bunny placed her hand over her mouth and studied Seth on his knees, ferns marking his trousers with damp streaks she'd have to remove with *Stain Away – We Promise to make Everything Good as New.*

AN EVALUATION OF SETH JOHNSON

Nose: There are strands of wire wool clinging to his cuffs. The steely scent of straight rows of paint pots mingles with the aroma of the sawdust that catches on his clothes. Outside the hardware store, he saws planks into lengths to fit into his customers' carts. Lifting a dusty hand, he says, 'No problem. No extra charge,' and waves people off to their homes in need of repair, lengths of timber and ladders sticking out of their vans.

Palate: He tastes of the casseroles various women from church kept bringing around after his wife passed away. Bunny Tyler stood out from the others. There was no pussyfooting around with her. She didn't treat his grief as something wrapped around him that would rub off if she brushed past it. She came in one day and pulled a boiled egg out of her handbag to demonstrate a slicing device he simply 'had to' stock. It seemed she always had what he needed in that bag of hers, bits of kitchenware that could lure fresh brides into the hardware store, solutions for paint stains he'd never heard of before, and a packet of candles. Twelve for the chocolate cake he'd bought for his son's birthday a year after his wife passed away. Seth hadn't felt like celebrating, but he'd bought the boy a chemistry set, blown up a few balloons and said, 'Make a wish, son,' praying he wouldn't say what he really wished for out loud.

Finish: A flannel-shirted species of man, the kind no one ever sees cry. The kind who returns a casserole dish without it being properly washed, a crust of gravy scorched to the lip. Watching the woman who brought him the meal, he'll wonder why she brought it, attempt to decipher her smile and have no idea what it means. In the end, he'll stop trying to figure out why she keeps stopping by. Bunny Tyler is a decent woman – small waist, light as air, decent cook. He's forty-one. Kindness is kindness. He'll take it wherever he can.

Overall: A man destined to be a husband. He appears occasionally to remember a time before he was married, sometimes in the store. Chatting to other men, organising a sly card game, he remembers a part of himself he forgets as soon as his son walks into the room. In the absence of being able to smile much himself following his wife's death, he clings to the smile of a well-meaning woman until it infects his own face and the boy's.

Bunny studied the beaming congregation and said 'Yes, I think. Yes!'

Everyone applauded. Women would applaud the beauty of it for years to come – the widow being lifted off her feet by the widower, being held by him, briefly, appropriately, outside the church. It was as close to romance as the island ever saw. Everyone would remember it. Nobody would remember the 'I think'.

Bunny pulled away from Seth's bristly kiss and laughed. People began to trail away to their Sundays, chicken and lamb in the oven and cabbage and potatoes peeled in water-filled pans. Sylvie wandered away from her mother shaking hands with the minister and discussing wedding plans. Finding some rice outside the church, she held out her palm to feed a limping pigeon on the wall. She made cooing sounds, trying to learn the language it spoke.

I didn't go over to her. I hadn't seen Sylvie all week, other than a glimpse on Sunday night. It had been late. Bunny's tyres shushed over the gravel and I looked out to see Sylvie stumbling out of the car. Bunny guided her in, lead-footed and sleepy as a child after a day at the seaside.

I could have knocked when she was off school the following week. Or brought her the latest issue of *Bunty*, but I didn't. Robin Macleod was teaching me elastics. She jumped, and criss-crossed, and wove with her feet, chatting about castrating ponies. She was the only girl in a family of four brothers. Her whole life was a competition; she ran as fast as a boy, spat as far, too, and made a point of being ruder and smarter. Rabbits meant nothing to me. I wanted a friend who could break in a horse.

'That Sylvie's always off.' Robin spat her distaste for meek girls out of her mouth. 'I hate people like her, acting shy and thinking they're better than everyone else.'

She whipped her elastics into her pocket and held out a hand. Other girls loved playing hopscotch or whispering in alcoves; Robin loved proving she was stronger than anyone else. We arm-wrestled and I felt myself give. I was barely trying, I didn't want to win.

Miss Jones called me over after class and gave me some work to drop off for Sylvie. I crumpled the pages and threw them into a hedgerow after school. I didn't want to stop at Sylvie's. I didn't feel like pushing anything through her letter box. I decided to let her fade into being no more than a pale face at a window next door.

Ma plops the rabbit on the bed. It honks of straw and wee. When it rests on my knee it's warm as damp mittens drying by the fire.

'Look who came to see you!' she says.

The rabbit's nibbling the bedspread. Ma's waiting for me to cuddle it, I know. I roll on my side. I won't look.

It's the only pet she ever named. Mr Churchill. But I can't love it like she does. When I was wee, the rabbits kept dying. Any rabbit could go any day. I reckon it's easier if I don't feel how fluffy they are.

'You still poorly, hen?' Ma's palm on my head feels for heat. 'You seem alright to me.'

'I'm a tad limp, that's all.'

I stand and wander to the window, all wobbly. But I'm tonnes better than I was when we left Nan's. Fit enough for church and school on Monday anyway.

The canary's puffed up into a ball in his cage. Outside, Lorrie's raking leaves. Toby keeps mussing up the pile, just to do her head in. I wave and he waves back. Lorrie ducks behind the shed.

'Lorrie doesn't pop over so much any more.' Ma peers over my shoulder. 'Have you had a falling-out?'

'Not exactly,' I say.

It's not as simple as falling out. Me and Lorrie don't have

to fall out. We never really fell in. It's pointless telling Ma. She ain't listening. She's dangling the rabbit in front of me and putting on her cutesy voice like a cartoon before the matinee.

'Hello missy, I want a cuddle with my favourite girl.'

She's making that lip-smacking sound like if rabbits could talk, they'd be pondering the joys of carrots all day long.

'Don't worry,' Ma says, in her own voice again. 'I'll smooth everything over with Lorrie. I'll go have a chat with her mother. I've got a fresh batch of kitchenware anyway. I have these lovely little pots for storing egg mayonnaise.' She pushes the rabbit towards me.

'Go on, take him. You know you want to.'

I know she won't go until she gets what she wants. She'll crawl in the attic and drag out Da's letters from the war. 'He was always so hungry,' she'll say. 'I didn't think the pantry could ever have enough to fill him when he came home.' She'll tell me about swapping her wedding dress for two rabbits. That became four, that became ten. Peace of mind she could hold in her arms for a while. I don't want to hear about his ribs ever again.

Whenever she tells me about Da, she's got this habit of stroking her wrist, like she's feeling the bones. 'He was so small, I could reach all the way around him and grip my own elbows.' I can't stand to see her showing me, her arms out in front of her. Holding on to nothing.

I stroke Mr Churchill and she shuts up. The fur's silky and cool. He's got this dip in his skull where my finger fits just right. It's so warm there and soft. Damn rabbit. And Ma, war and friends. I'm too shattered to think about it all.

'Don't worry about anything,' she's saying. 'I'll make everything right.'

The rabbit's dangling in front of me. I breathe in the straw on its huge fluffy feet, and the furry scent that reminds me of sleep. I hold him so close I can feel his tiny heart beat through my fingers. His nose twitching on my lips. Ma whispers 'That's my girl', and slips her arm around me, holding me up as I droop and shuffle back to bed.

Bunny arrived with pie and a smile. The cottage was in chaos. The cabinets lay in splinters by the door. The freshly plastered walls left a rosy dust on our clothes. Grumps saw Bunny, mumbled, 'fucking hell', and ducked out the back door. He returned to the distillery with a sandwich and the sense of having avoided something painful. For forty years, his wife dealt with the pleasantries to neighbours. In company, he did the listening, she did the talking. It worked. When she passed away, she left him all listening and never quite knowing what to say.

Bunny fussed with Sylvie's hair and curled a strand behind her ear.

'Don't slouch,' she hissed, turning to beam at my mother opening the door. 'Hello, I thought it was time I came over to officially introduce myself,' she said. 'Sylvie, get your hair out of your mouth. Girls!'

She offered a handshake at the sort of angle Victorian ladies may present a hand to be kissed, balancing a pie in the other.

'Come in,' Mum said. 'Sorry about the mess.'

If the words on headstones were the phrases people spoke the most in their lives *I'm sorry about the mess* would be carved on hers. *I'm sorry I'm here* would be on Sylvie's. I wasn't sure what mine would be yet.

AN EVALUATION OF MY MOTHER

Nose: The clothes she wears have the slightest aroma of the dust she sweeps around the kitchen, spilled sugar, beeswax and coffee. Her breath has a hint of hops and ice cream, remnants of the small treats she dangles to get herself through the day. 'As soon as I finish cleaning the kitchen, painting this wall, hanging the laundry out . . . I'm going to sit still for fifteen minutes.' She is one of those women who must always have something in her hands. It's the only way she can stop them clearing something away.

Palate: The bread she bakes that only rises fifty per cent of the time, strands of cotton she sucks and threads through a needle to sew on all our buttons. Her little finger tastes of whisky. She dips it into a shot glass at the distillery on bottling days, refusing to drink during daylight. It always reminds her of being a child, she says, the marmalade her mother made for everyone at Christmas, a splash of whisky in a jar bright as fire.

Finish: Freckled in summer, the weather brings out chestnut stripes in her hair. Left to her own devices, she'd never wear shoes. She wants her feet and legs bare. Whenever she hears a car or footsteps outside, she dashes to the mirror before anyone comes in. Bunny knocks and she slips on her shoes and runs her hands over her hair, doing her best to appear formal and neat and how she thinks a woman is supposed to be.

Overall: Mother with a dash of girl thrown in that no amount of herringbone skirts, sensible trousers or cable-knit jumpers can disguise.

Bunny wiped the chair with a handkerchief and sat. The kettle boiled while the pair chatted about the weather, the

Quaker family who lived in Bunny's house before my mother left home ('beautiful people, faces plain as white bread') and me being a lovely girl. I didn't want to be lovely. I wanted them to leave.

'Congratulations on your engagement,' Mum said. 'It must have been difficult, being on your own.'

Bunny swatted away sympathy faster than flies from a pie.

'It could have been worse. I wasn't alone. I have Sylvie.'

She gave Sylvie a look I hadn't seen on her before. It gave the impression the girl was something other than a nuisance who kept too much junk in her pockets (feathers she found, interestingly shaped stones, the small skull of a bird picked clean by the gulls).

'I didn't think we could have children,' Bunny said. 'Sylvie was our miracle.'

'Miracle' was Bunny's favourite word. Miracle Tile Cleaner, Miracle Scissors that claim to cut a coin in half, the Miracle Apple Peeler. The Miracle Boots that saved her husband's life.

I'd heard the story before, but she told it again. It was amazing Sylvie was born. John Tyler was almost killed in the war. Gunfire pelted his squad. They ran for cover, only finding the bullet that hit him later. He found it lodged in his boots, knotted by the laces and hung over his shoulder.

'If it wasn't for the steel plate in the soles he'd have died years before Sylvie was born. She wouldn't be here at all,' Bunny said. Three years later he'd died anyway, searching the loft for mousetraps, he coughed until something in his head popped. As far as miracles go, I thought it was shoddy.

Bunny dusted sugar off her cup and turned her attention to the kitchen.

'Will you have that pie after supper?' She nodded at the baking on the table.

'Would you like a slice now?' My mother's knife hovered.

'Heavens, no, by the time I've made something I'm sick of the sight of it! That's the one thing no one admits about cooking. It only tastes good when someone else did it.'

'Well, it was kind of you to bring it anyway. As you can see, we have our work cut out for us.'

They looked at the spaces where the cabinets had been. The carpenter's horse was braced for their replacements. The pie was blackberry with frosty sugared pastry.

'How long ago do you think I baked this?' Bunny asked.

'This morning?'

'Yesterday, yet it's still so fresh. Did you know there's more bacteria in your kitchen than in a dog's mouth? It's up to you to fight germs and provide your family with the best. You can be confident storing food in plastic, even with leftovers. The pots come in any size you could imagine . . . '

Bunny's crusade against stale crusts and limp lettuce began. She pulled out a brochure.

'Why don't you go play with your friend, Lorrie?' My mother's eyes said: It's too late for me, go, save yourself. I winced at her use of the word 'friend', it was a leash around my neck, tying me to Sylvie. I'd rather have been somewhere else.

The dust drifted on the stairs, the air full of fibres. Another shoal of silverfish had been evicted last week. I opened my door and sneezed.

'This is it, my bedroom. They haven't decorated yet.'

I sniffed and sneezed again.

'I keep wondering if there are more dead things under the floor.'

Sylvie stroked the roses on the wall, a patch of colour on the flowers so much brighter than the others. I'd taken down the pictures my mother pinned up as a child. They were all circus scenes: elephants, ballerinas dancing on horses, and women with lions. I kept only the photo I found under the floor. It was my mother at sixteen, piggybacking a young man with coal-black hair. His hands circled her ankles, holding her firm. Her arms looped around his neck, casual as a sweater. They were grinning. They were grinning so much that once the photo was taken they'd probably have fallen into a heap laughing. I wanted to ask about it, but somehow I never quite got around to it. My mother always had so much to clean and unpack there was never room to drag out the life she'd lived before I was born.

Sylvie stroked a tea chest labelled 'Bits and Bobs'. I sneezed again.

'You've got allergies? Germs?' she said. 'You know what your problem is? You don't have enough Tupperware. Did you know there are more germs in your bed than a cat's arse?'

She grinned a wicked little grin, a glimpse of a whole other side to her she'd never showed me before. *If she was always like that*, I thought, *we'd get on*. It was gone in a flash.

'What shall we do? I've got roller skates . . . '

I glanced towards the clouds darkening fast as a bruise.

'It's going to rain. I've got board games somewhere.'

I sliced some sticky tape off a box and tossed Snakes and Ladders onto the bed. 'Do you like the guy your mother's marrying?' I asked.

'Seth? I suppose so. He's alright,' Sylvie said.

This was a glowing review, 'they're alright' was the most glowing review I'd heard anyone on the island give anyone. Compliments were spat out as reluctantly as saying the weather looked fine; acknowledging anything was OK was tempting fate. As soon as anyone said something was great, it could only get worse. Seth deserved the praise, Sylvie said, because he let her put her rag doll in a wheelbarrow when she was little. He didn't care when she knocked over a display of buckets and crashed into a customer buying a snow shovel. She could wheel that barrow up and down all she wanted. It didn't bother him at all. It added laughter to the store. He could stand more.

'I love the way he is with Ma,' Sylvie said. 'She sort of turns into someone else when he comes in, someone softer. When she's complaining about me being shy at dinner, or sucking my knuckles, he just rolls his eyes. Let the girl be. The stiller the water, the deeper the river, he says. Better to say little than a whole load of nothing.'

'He says that to Bunny?!'

Sylvie laughed.

'Aye, all the time. He does this funny wee wink when she's giving me grief, like he's on my side, and he can see Ma's annoying and love her at the same time. It's more bearable living with her when he's around, but . . . ' Sylvie slid a counter up a ladder. 'I'm worried that . . . '

Bunny's voice sing-songed upstairs.

'Come on, Sylvie, we should make a move. I've got a kitchen gadget demonstration at the Women's Institute. I want you to come and peel tatties the wrong way while I show them mashed potato will never be the same again.'

Bunny and Sylvie left. I sat with my mother opening and closing the storage pot she had bought. There was nowhere to store it. It was too small to hold anything that could fill anyone up.

'I'm not sure what to put in it,' my mother said.

It would happen the same way as the dentists. Every so often, that time came again when we had to put on a scarf, sail to the mainland and return with numb jaws and a tooth in our pocket. Just as inevitably, every so often Bunny would arrive with a container full of gingerbread and a brochure, leaving my mother with a sweet taste in her mouth and no change in her purse. 'She got me again,' she'd say. 'I don't know how she does it! I never use a thing I buy off her.'

The women were courteous without ever truly liking each other. They swapped recipes and magazines, Bunny grumbling about flour crusted to the pages whenever a cookbook was returned, my mother noting Bunny had snipped out the contest to win a fridge out of *Woman's Own*. We weren't country people. In the city, it was easy to like and dislike our neighbours. We liked the man who scraped dandelions out of the footpath, and disliked the woman who never picked up after her Jack Russell, and took in parcels for both. Everyone could be smiled at and waved away to their own lives with a 'lovely morning' or a 'nice weather for ducks'. It wasn't so simple on the island. My mother had to get used to jam-making competitions, being ambushed by pies and everyone knowing everyone's business. I had to live with the realisation Sylvie and I would be friends. It was impossible not to be.

I'd probably have drifted away from Robin Macleod anyway, because of spit. Robin had just seen a film where some boys became blood brothers, and since neither of us were about to cut our hands, she said we could do it with spit. I looked at her palm covered with a puddle of bubbles, waiting to be pressed against mine. I lowered my head over her hand and found my mouth dry. I couldn't bring myself to do it. I suggested we make a friendship bracelet instead.

'You're the same as everyone else,' she said. 'A girly girl. Scared to do anything in case you get dirty.'

Robin flipped me the Vs and stormed off. I settled on Sylvie. Compared to her I always looked brave. She made me look like I could do anything.

I can hear everything changing. The furniture shuffling all over the place. The sofa and the armchair pushing their backs to the wall. Another sofa squeezes into the lounge and our footsteps rustle, the floor covered in paper. Ma's sewing room's getting a lick of blue paint to make it fit for a boy. It won't be long until Seth moves in with his son, Zach. Ma can't stop moving. All day and night she scurries around, hiding anything too girly like kryptonite that will kill a lad on sight.

The button box must go. The lacy pillows and all. The ornaments. Even those china milkmaids she loves rearranging on the dresser cower in the loft, folded in paper like lasses having a kip.

Ma stomps the bronze boots on my dresser. *Thud!* It doesn't feel right letting them kick about downstairs when another fella's shoes are on the mat. She's taken Our Lady off the shelf too, and plonks it down with the Bible we keep by the bog.

'It's not that Seth hates church,' she says. 'He has nothing against Our Lady. He just doesn't want to feel her staring at him all day. Religion's like cabbage, he says, he knows a bit of it's good for him, but he doesn't want it for every meal.'

Ma laughs, all love and nerves and fearty, scared to death of letting folks into our life. It's been just me and her for so long we dunno how to be with anyone else. 'You know, things are going to be different around here,' she keeps saying.

The place is reeking of the smoked fish in the soup she's got bubbling downstairs. She's wearing camellia perfume. And she's achieved those feathery flicks in her hair. I know Seth's gonna arrive any minute because she looks like a catalogue woman.

'I'm not sure it's sensible to get married,' she says, 'but . . .'

I know what the but is . . . she gets lonely. The kind of lonely no amount of face masks or beating me at dominoes can cure.

'Do you think it's a mistake?' she says. 'He's a sweet man.'

'I just want you to be happy,' I say. 'It'll be alright.'

I dunno if it will be, but it's what she wants to hear. It's not that much of a shock she's engaged. I reckon nothing's been the same since the Sausage Wizard arrived and she did a meat-grinding demonstration outside the hardware store. I sorta knew this day would happen. It's been coming for years. And it still feels dead sudden now it's finally here.

Ma strokes my hair. Quietly, and knowing the quiet is as frail as china with cracks. Seth's already here. Knock knock knocking. He's lunging through the door with a massive stack of records slipping and sliding out of his arms. His toolbox is already on the floor in the living room. By the time they get married we'll have enough shelves for Nat King Cole.

'Bunny? Can I shift this table?' he calls.

'I'm coming!'

Ma skips towards his voice like a lassie who hasn't skipped for a year.

'Don't move anything without me! I know where everything should go!'

She pauses at the door wanting to say more, but she can't. The place is too full. Full of fish stink, and screwdrivers, and wrenches and screws, and her own voice telling her man to be careful where he leaves his tools. It's jam-packed with the life she wants to live. I reckon I know what she wants to say anyway. Everything will be different soon. When the lads come, we've got to be careful about certain things. There are eyes and ears everywhere.

LORRIE

Bunny married on a Saturday in spring. The parachute strung across the garden to provide an awning billowed. The stocks she'd planted crawled with bees. Every woman who owned a kitchen gadget or man who'd bought a hammer within a five-mile radius attended in their squeakiest shoes. 'There's no need for a fuss at my age,' Bunny would say, setting about her plans with military precision. The plans went on for months, with more guests being added to the list every day. Seth kept inviting his customers to 'pop in' to the reception: 'No need to bother with church first, if it's not your sort of thing. Just come for a bite to eat and to raise a glass.' It was a hell of a month for business. Seth's customers left with screws and promises of cake almost as good as a discount. Bunny smacked his arm in the post office. 'There you go, inviting the world and his dog! Where will we put everyone? You'd better set to work on my lawn, mister. You've invited more than will fit in the house!'

Seth set about weeding Bunny's borders. My father wandered outside to catch him on his own before the wedding the following week.

'Nice to meet you. We'll be neighbours soon.'

He shook Seth's hand and inspected his own, suddenly aware of how soft it must seem. Those hands had known nothing but paperwork and pens until they'd arrived on the island. Now, they knew nothing but waving people onto a ferry for their journey, and waving them off, back and forth all day. I never saw a man who smiled so little wave so much. Seth leant on his rake, my father struggling to make conversation. He knew nothing about hardware. He struggled to put up a shelf.

'I suppose we will be neighbours.'

Seth pulled a dandelion and tossed it in a bucket.

'I was thinking, perhaps I could join your card game?'

My father did his best to sound laid-back and didn't quite pull it off.

Seth glanced towards the distillery, contemplating my grandfather's disapproval. A bet was a serious matter, no one knew that more than Grumps. He wouldn't want his son-in-law in the game he'd participated in for years. Bad enough sharing a house with him. Friday nights had always been a night off from family. Besides, never play cards with a man who can't crack a joke, can't be trusted.

'We have a full game right now.' Seth picked up a stone. It clanked into his bucket. He lowered his voice. Not everyone knew about the cards. He wanted to keep it that way.

'But if someone drops out in the future, who knows? I can do you a discount at the store though. How's that? Now we're neighbours: screws, tools, paint. Anything you need.'

It meant nothing. Grumps hadn't paid full price for hardware in years. He virtually owned that store. Then he didn't, then he did. Every weekend the same group of men played in Seth's stockroom, surrounded by last season's hoses and shovels. Seth Johnson won Grumps' pick-up once. Grumps won Seth's. The men got to display their largesse by letting their friends keep their cars and agreeing to play for same stakes next week. They would laugh and wave at one another across the street. 'Be careful how you load that coal! I own that car until Friday night . . . I'll be there with bells on. Careful, or you'll be walking home!'

I could always tell when Grumps won by the way he walked: straighter, with a glint in his eye, sharp as a boy sneaking a sip from a hip flask under moonlight. I could also tell when he lost. He'd sit in the distillery doorway: head low, staring at a dead owl he'd found outside. The slightest win could make a man a decade younger, or strip the spring out of his stride. I supposed that was why my father wanted in.

'Congratulations anyway, congratulations.'

My father repeated himself, unsure he had said it right the first time. I don't know how he managed to make such a joyous word sound so flat, but he did. He had a voice that could suck the air out of anything. Thinking about it, there wasn't much he managed to make sound joyous, but I barely noticed. None of us did.

AN EVALUATION OF MY FATHER

Nose: He carries the aroma of his desk covered in paperclip chains, ink from the pen that spots his shirt pocket, and the cigarettes he can't smoke in front of men like my grandfather without looking ashamed. The men who were born here hold a cigarette differently, clamped between forefinger and thumb. They snip out the fire with the tips of their fingers. My father's cigarette perches in the V of his fingers, in a Hollywood manner. He scours the ashtrays longer than most, until he is sure nothing glows.

Palate: The ham and mustard sandwiches he gets out of the same brown bag every day, tipping yesterday's crumbs away. His favourite food is the gooseberry crumble my mother makes for his birthday every year, and the hot chocolate he occasionally orders in cafés to remind my mother of the day they met. He looks at his wife, letting the foam on the top of the milk linger for a second, hoping to invite her finger to his lips. Eventually, he wipes it off himself.

Finish: Brown as sparrows. Black jackets and trousers are under-takers' clothes. His former career selling insurance made him cautious. He didn't want to remind his clients of a vulture when he asked them to picture their families paying for their funerals. Almost everything he owns is dark blue or brown. There's one sheep-coloured sweater in his wardrobe my mother bought him when he complained about the wind on the island. I saw him wear it only once. The whole time he looked scared of gravy. He is a man who lacks the ability to put on anything that could stain.

Overall: He's a man passing through, small villages, kitchens, swigging milk on his way out the door and onto the road that once brought him to my mother. He had come to the island to scatter his parents' ashes and found a girl. Eighteen, sitting in a café by the port, alone, head full of dreams. 'Where are you heading?' she asked. 'The mainland. Do you want to come along for the ride?' he said. It was a joke. He didn't tell jokes well. She looked towards the silent road, at the person she'd agreed to meet failing to approach and said, 'I do', as spontaneous as the journey was planned. A trip to the mainland wouldn't hurt. It had been a while.

He didn't shave for the wedding. My father moved through the crowd stroking his stubble, attempting to rub his soft edges away. Bunny hosted her reception outside. It was one of those island mornings where the horizon brightens and fades and every other sentence is about the chances of rain. The clouds were biblical. They appeared to be painted-on silver. Everyone looked up, cradling their drinks, wondering if they should go inside. The sun didn't show until lunchtime.

It was brighter at the front of the cottage. In the garden, folding chairs perched on the grass, yellow cloths fluttering around the legs of the picnic tables Seth assembled himself. Bunny had been cooking all week. Our cold store overflowed with surplus salad, fishcakes, langoustines and a special tartar sauce she absolutely refused to share the recipe for. 'You must give me the secret to those fishcakes,' women said. 'You made those tables? I couldn't have done better myself,' the men told her husband. They loosened their ties, freed from church, while their wives slipped off their party shoes beneath the tables and rubbed their bare feet on freshly cut grass. Bunny was a whirlwind, complimenting the outfits of her guests, filling up glasses, and flitting to the kitchen for more bread.

'Guess how long ago I made this?' she said. 'I had no time this morning, with getting ready and doing Sylvie's hair. That child! Nothing but tangles! I made the bread yesterday, yet it's still so fresh.'

Not even in a pillbox hat and an ivory suit with a whisper of ermine on the collar could she quite drop her sales pitch. It was an occasion to celebrate love, food, drink, home repair and kitchenware. The crowd raised their glasses and tapped their feet, the fiddler on the lawn sawing a dance out of usually stern-faced old men. The wives laughed, grabbing their husbands to stop them making fools of themselves. Oh, why not? They staggered into familiar arms, swirled into a foxtrot. Everyone looked happy, except Sylvie. All she wanted was to disappear.

It was killing her, the fun, all the noise. People everywhere, stopping to compliment the violets looped to her wrist with a ribbon, or comment on how much she'd grown. She rubbed her neck again and again. It ached from lowering her head for so long, trying to look less tall.

'What do you enjoy in school?' Her grandma ferreted in her bag.

She was a small weasel-faced woman who'd come over from Mull. Her fingers clawed a cigarette out of the packet. She lit it with a wince.

'Is your arthritis playing up again Mammy?' Bunny asked. 'Perhaps you want to lie down in Sylvie's room?'

Sylvie scratched her knuckles. During the ceremony, she'd stood with her mother where a father may give away his daughter. Now she was less sure of her place.

'Sylvie! Answer your Nan! Tell her what your favourite subjects at school are!'

'I don't enjoy anything at school, other than when it's over,' Sylvie said, jerking away from Bunny's hand on her forearm.

'You'll have to forgive her, you know she's shy,' Bunny said.

'She'll grow out of it, I used to be shy. It's a phase.'

'*Everyone* was shy,' Sylvie whispered, looping her arm into mine. 'That's what they all say. It's a lie.'

We wandered around searching for a quiet spot to make our own party. We planned on grabbing a bowl of crisps, the icing and none of the fruit cake, and a bottle of cola with a waxy straw.

The cottage was packed. There was nowhere to go. The alcove where Sylvie loved to sit with a book was occupied by a woman stuffing tissues into shoes that pinched her heels. The lounge heaved with chuckles at an anecdote about changing rooms given by a large woman in a dress that almost fit. Sylvie slipped out of the door. I followed, waylaid by Toby trying to show me his magic. Today was his chance to be a star. He grinned, covering ping pong balls with cups in the kitchen, finally in the presence of someone who hadn't seen his act before.

'How did you do that?' Seth's son asked.

Zach was a couple of years older than me. I knew little of him, other than he worked in his father's store at weekends, mixing paint in a way that put Michelangelo to shame.

Zach looked at me and asked, 'Do you know any tricks, Lorrie?'

I smiled with nothing up my sleeve.

'Looks like a good trick.'

He stirred a jug of blackcurrant cordial smooth as a pot of emulsion. The quiet way he carried himself rendered me unable to pull myself away. A girl would never be able to tell what he was thinking, even if she looked at him for a hundred years. I could look for a hundred years without getting bored. He was easy to watch. I imagined marrying him for a second, looking at him was practice for something I wasn't ready for yet.

'See you later.' I smiled and went outside to find Sylvie.

It was quiet in the back garden. All day, Bunny had been ushering guests away. The rabbit hutches and chicken runs would be scruffy on the photos. The borders bustled with too many unruly wild flowers Sylvie begged Seth to let stay. It was just me and Sylvie. She was bending down, peering into a foxglove to watch a bee sleep. The chickens were scratching about. The white one she loved pecked about by itself, then stopped in a blur.

The cat leapt off the fence. Claws out, canines biting through skin. The bird screeched and fell quiet, blood spraying from its neck. Sylvie rushed to it flapping her arms, a flush of colour gushing to her cheeks, panic darting in her eyes. *Hsssssss*. The cat hissed and squeezed through the fence. Sylvie knelt down to stroke the chicken on the grass. It lay on the ground stunned. She placed a palm on the wound, feathers floating around. I could see the bird breathing, its plump chest slowly moving and down. It barely made a sound.

'Sylvie?' I whispered.

She didn't turn around. One hand on a wing, she lowered her head and placed her lips on the bird's neck. I stared at her open-mouthed. It reminded me of when I came into the kitchen and caught my mother with the plumber. They'd be doing nothing but chatting, but I felt I was interrupting something. Mum would be wearing lipstick though she wasn't going anywhere. The fawn shoes she loved slipped on and off one heel, legs crossed, facing him, sipping coffee at the table. I saw I shouldn't be there; whatever I'd walked in on was a moment for them alone. This moment belonged to only one girl and a bird.

Sylvie looked up, blood on her chin, feathers crusted to her lace collar. The blood was already drying on her hands, and falling in flakes, freckling her skirt. *Bok bok bok bawk.* The chicken flapped up with an indignant shriek.

'It's not dead?' I said. 'It's not dead!'

I stared at the bird, pecking the ground with the other chickens now. I was sure it had been so badly injured all I could say to Sylvie was 'I'm sorry', or 'snap its neck', if it didn't die quickly. It was alive. Sylvie got up and wandered to the bench with a sway reminiscent of a party guest who'd raised one toast too many.

'That bird was done for,' I said. 'It looked . . . '

'Worse than it was.' Sylvie smiled at the bird, her eyes closing softly.

'Sylvie? Sylvie? Heavens, where is that child?'

The kitchen door flung open and Bunny burst out of it waving.

'Come on! We're taking a group picture out front!'

The words congealed in Bunny's mouth. She gasped at the sight of us: two girls. One in a powder-blue dress. One in a lemon dress sprayed with blood, dirt on her knees and feathers in her hair. Sylvie stretched her cardigan, attempting to hide the stains, and gave in. There was no disguising anything.

'What the . . . ?'

Bunny glanced at the door, aware of the party behind her. The forks clinking glasses waiting for a speech, the gifts that all looked suspiciously like teapots waiting to be opened. The photographs weren't all taken yet. Thirsty people needed drinks. The fun depended on her.

'What have you done? Today of all days, Sylvie! You're filthy. The photos! What will it look like?'

Bunny grabbed Sylvie by the shoulders and attempted to shake the dazed look off her face.

'It's not her fault, Mrs Tyler, I mean, Mrs Johnson, Mrs . . . Bunny. It was that crazy wildcat. It pounced on the chicken. Sylvie had to . . . '

I stopped. I had no idea what Sylvie had to do.

The photographer came out mopping his brow, all ready to say 'cheese'.

'Where's that bride and the bridesmaid? We won't have this light for long!'

He squinted through a viewfinder, clicked and froze where he stood. This was the photograph no one wanted to frame: Bunny yelling at Sylvie, a streak of cotton, feathers and blood.

In a blink, Bunny stepped out of the picture and became who she wanted the man holding the camera to see. The hostess. The doting mother. The bride.

'Kids! What can you do? They're always playing in the dirt!' Bunny smiled. 'There's a clean dress in your wardrobe, Sylvie, petal. Get changed.'

The woman squeezed my shoulder. 'Will you help her get ready, Lorrie? I think she's eaten a dodgy winkle or had a shandy or something.'

Bunny ushered the photographer inside. I held out my arm for Sylvie. She stood and leant on me, so light, yet barely able to support herself.

'The peachy dress, not the white one!' Bunny yelled. 'And wash your face!'

I followed Sylvie upstairs, one or two wedding guests on their way out of the bathroom turning to stare.

'What on earth . . . ? Is that blood?'

People gasped at the girl who appeared to have been working in an abattoir. Bunny ushered them out to the lawn.

'Just a little accident with spilled cordial! Nothing to worry about! Now, let's get you another drink.'

Years later, at school, sometimes someone would raise an eyebrow and say, 'Sylvie Johnson's your friend? Isn't she the one who bit a bird's neck at a christening or something?' 'No,' I'd reply. 'That's what I heard . . . ' they'd say.

I'd attempt to defend her, but it never quite worked. The story lived on without me. I'd sometimes hear schoolgirls whispering it without being sure who was involved. *Did you hear about the girl who whispered to chickens? I heard she lives around here. I heard she could make birds do anything she wants them to . . . That's not what I heard, I heard there's some lassie who drinks chicken blood to live forever. She's a hundred years old, but she looks just like us. She could be anywhere, she could be in our class, watching us.*

Whenever I asked Sylvie about it, she'd simply shrug. 'It wasn't that bad. It was only a scratch. The chicken was fine. You're squeamish, that's all.' The more I tried to explain it, the less I could. I wasn't sure what really happened. 'Sylvie's alright,' I'd snap at anyone who asked. I didn't trust my memory of feathers. Sylvie must have picked up the wounded bird to see if it was OK. That's all, I persuaded myself. It couldn't have been anything like I remembered, I was sure, until I wasn't any more.

PART II

Ma's carrying the cake with wee footsteps like a geisha. I'm wincing and picturing her dropping it. The candles drip waxy puddles all over the icing and I gulp a breath. Hold it in. The older I get the more I need to learn to breathe. Sixteen little fires looks like a lot to put out.

'Happy Birthday!'

Ma's singing and nudging Lorrie to join in.

'You too, boys!'

Zach and Seth mumble-sing like they're being made to say the Lord's Prayer. Their eyes fix on the cake and their stomachs gurgle for a slice. The zing of lemon drizzle hangs in the air. Everyone's staring and waiting for me to look all happy and stuff. I pucker and blow. Face burning for everyone to look at something else. *Whoosh!* The flames wobble out.

'Did you make a wish?' Lorrie's asking.

'Of course I did.'

Ma looks away. Only she knows what it is. It's the same wish I've been making since I was a wean. Let me be the same as everyone else, God, please. Let me grow out of being different.

The knife splits the sponge dead centre. Ma cuts a strip and pushes both halves of the cake together. Folks who cut cakes pie chart style make her die a wee bit. They've got it all wrong. It's a stinking waste of a cake. She can't watch folk slice a Victoria sponge without waggling a finger. 'No! You're doing it wrong! It will never stay fresh. The ends will dry out! No!'

Lorrie passes me a package knotted with string.

'It's just a little something.'

Everyone's all eyes, gawking at me and the gift. I don't want to open it. I love gifts, and I hate them. I hate the way they make folk gawp to see what my face is gonna do. I'm supposed to look happy and jump up and down. I want to, but I'm not sure I look surprised right. Before the party, Zach gave me this book called *Everything You Ever Needed to Know in the Universe*. It's fat as a brick and stuffed with facts. After they found his Ma, he couldn't stop reading it, he said. He started learning a funny fact every day. One, two, three, four, sometimes ten, he'd memorise as many as he could. Just wanting to know everything. I loved the gift, but I couldn't say anything before Zach said, 'It's shite. I just couldn't be arsed to get you a real present.' *Pouf!* He was off to his bedroom, our sibling moment vanished in a flash. I blame my face. It's not right, when it's supposed to look grateful it only looks constipated.

Lorrie's present's too bonnie to open anyway. She wraps most stuff like a lassie forced to wear mittens all day long. Scrunching the ends of paper, twisting it round, boiled sweet style. Today, she's tried to do it properly. Just for me.

I can feel Ma nosing over my shoulder, her interest turned up like the volume on the *Calamity Jane* soundtrack. Seth was supposed to take us to the mainland to see it a couple of years ago, but we all got snowed in. By the time the snow thawed, it wasn't at the cinema any more. He bought Ma the soundtrack instead. She puts it on whenever she does the dusting. One day she'll see the film. I doubt it can be as good as the one in her head. And just like when she's singing along, she keeps smiling. I unwrap the present and hold up a pearly shell compact and lipstick. The shell is so cool in my hand I kinda want to press it against my cheeks.

'You girls!' Ma shakes her head. 'I don't know why you feel you need all that stuff. Honestly, if God had thought your smiles weren't colourful enough he'd have painted your lips scarlet himself.'

She rubs a peachy smudge her mouth has left on her lemonade glass and starts folding the gift wrap. I spool up the string to use again.

'Perhaps I could just wear it on special occasions, Ma?' I say. 'Just a smidge now and then?'

'Cake?'

She passes a saucer to Lorrie.

'Sylvie has such sensitive skin. She has to be careful what she puts on her face. It was very sweet of you anyway, Lorrie. It's the thought that counts,' she says.

And I know I'll never be allowed to wear the lipstick. Ever. Lorrie can show me how to apply it until the cows come home. And it won't make no difference.

Last time Lorrie dolled me up, I looked in the mirror and laughed until I almost weed. It was so funny. I saw me, kinda, but not me, a whole other version. Me, if I'd been born somewhere else and knew stuff like how to speak French. The difference was like the outlines of a lassie in a colouring book, compared to one who's been coloured in.

'You're a bonnie lass, Lorrie,' Ma says, picking up the lipstick and squirrelling it away. 'You'd look even lovelier if you wore less make-up and let your natural beauty shine.'

'You should give me some tips on invisible make-up some time, Bunny,' Lorrie says.

Ma smiles. And Lorrie smiles back. They lock eyes, then both look at me. *Boom!* It's the prettiest declaration of war anyone ever saw. And I'm caught smack dab in the centre of it.

LORRIE

Seth Johnson took it on the chin when his wife found God. He'd always been there, solid as a worker who clocked in, did his job and never asked for a pay rise. But the year Sylvie turned sixteen Bunny gave him a promotion. It was noticeable in the smallest ways, everywhere. In the years that had passed since I'd arrived on the island, Sylvie had changed. We were no longer children, nor were we adults. The dolls we once had were pushed into our attics. The babies that women not much older than us pushed in weatherproof prams were far from our minds. Yet we could feel it, a sense of having to grow up closing in. Girls our age were already dressing for the part. They wore their mother's petticoats under pleated skirts, tried on dresses and experimented with rollers, covering their creations under yellow sou'wester hats and duffel coats. Sylvie was still wearing a vest while the rest of us fidgeted with our bra straps. Bunny kept her dressed in the same sort of clothes she'd worn as a child. She gave her a small silver cross and chain that nestled under the collar of a blouse at least two sizes too big for her. Everything she wore swamped her. I never heard Sylvie complain, but it must have bothered her. I didn't realise until we caught her with the magazines.

It was almost dark when my mother heard something outside. She looked out and saw Sylvie ferreting through a stack of magazines she'd left by the bin. The drizzle landed on her hair and stayed there. The rain was getting heavier, but Sylvie didn't care. I was used to seeing her on her knees, pausing to inspect some wounded creature on the ground, but not like this. In the presence of fallen fledglings she remained calm, now she was frantic. I stared over my mother's shoulder, unable to bring myself to go out. I was in my pyjamas, but that wasn't really why. I cringed at the sight of my friend scrabbling through the things we'd thrown away. My mother went to see what was wrong. Sylvie stuffed a magazine into her pocket and froze, eyes round and wild.

'What was she doing out there?' I asked.

'Looking through my magazines,' my mother said, bolting the door. 'Poor thing looked mortified I saw her. Bunny won't allow women's magazines in the house, Sylvie said. She claims they're not suitable for a child. Bunny reads plenty though! Just last week, I saw her buy four magazines for the contest to win a fridge. God, I hate the way the woman speaks to her. Stand up straight! Stop fidgeting, Sylvie! Look up! I want to shout, "Leave her alone, Bunny! Your daughter's not a dog." But it's not my place. Besides, it's hard to argue with someone who has a smile on their face.'

'You tell me not to slouch,' I said.

'Not that much. Put me on a diet, if I say it more than once a week poke me in the ribs.'

I poked her in the ribs and she allowed it to turn into a tickling fit until my father came in. He was long-faced, with his hands hanging at his sides, heavy from waving cars to their spots, crossing the same stretch of water again and again.

Bunny sailed into the hardware store a week later. I'd been pleading with Sylvie to come to the harbour and have a cola in the café facing the waves, but she wouldn't. Every Thursday

Sylvie insisted on staying late after school to organise the shelves in the library. I could never persuade her to skip it, not even if it was sunny and we had pocket money. She took alphabetising seriously.

'I have to sort fiction today,' she said. 'It's the least I can do. The librarian saved my life once. I didn't even thank her.'

'How?' I asked.

'Oh, it doesn't matter. It was a daft thing when I was little.' The watch she'd swapped with Zach slipped around on her bony wrist as she inspected the time. 'I have to go,' she said.

I walked on alone, stopping at the hardware store on the way. The store was my favourite place to kill time. Looking in, I spotted my father inside staring at the light bulbs, eavesdropping on the conversations of men at the counter without joining in.

'What you doing here?' I asked. 'I thought you were at work.'

'I had to go to the dentist.' He prodded his jaw. 'Poke it if you want. I can't feel a thing.'

We looked at one another, unsure why we felt like strangers caught doing something we shouldn't, uncertain what to talk about.

'What brings you here anyway? Do you want a lift? I have the car.'

'Not really, I've got something I have to get for a school project,' I said.

'Oh.'

We fell quiet. If he noticed I was wearing blusher on a weekday he didn't tell my mother. It's possible he had no idea it was only allowed on weekends. Just as I had no idea not a single light bulb had blown in the house and he had no real reason to be there.

'I love the smell of this place,' he said. 'Beeswax, varnish and pine.'

'I love it too. I love the fresh paint.'

'Well, I suppose I'll see you later then.' He left without buying anything.

I strolled around the store, sticking out my chest and taking my time to browse the aisles. I knew those aisles full of screws, nails and dowels the way some women know the perfume stand at the chemist. The aroma here was more alluring. I raked through a box of brass hooks, licking my lips and staring at Zach. Zach had worked at the paint counter full-time since he'd left school. He was nineteen now. He had a wave on his fringe that made me think a calf had licked his head, and eyelashes longer than a cow. He ran his finger along a colour chart, reassuring a lady clutching a swatch of tartan he could mix paint to match her curtains. I pictured strolling over, dropping my underwear on the counter and seeing if he could mix paint the same shade of peach. I imagined he'd blush, then get on with the job. Looking at Zach, I could picture a lot of things.

'Can I help you?' he asked me.

The woman walked to the door, promising to return to collect her Heather gloss on Monday.

'I'm just looking,' I met his eye. 'I'll know what I want when I see it.'

I jangled a hook out of the box. Whenever Zach spoke to me, I made a point of screwing a hook inside my wardrobe door. I had twelve now, all in line, dangling belts and scarves in the dark. Zach still hadn't asked me out. I was starting another row.

I lingered, listening to the men with calluses on their fingers loitering by the counter, comparing ways to build a fence. The store was a sewing circle of hammers, nails and complaints about the old ball and chain. Seth's inability to rush his customers was the real reason they returned more often than they needed to. Here, a man could spend an hour in a sawdust-scented world away from the wife, and, while he was at it, get some advice on foxes and chicken wire.

Bunny came in and the store bell jangled behind her.

'Good afternoon.'

The men lowered their heads, touching their caps, suddenly sheepish and tense.

AN EVALUATION OF BUNNY JOHNSON

Nose: She carries the scent of camellia and the gingerbread she rolls. Feeling unable to waste those leftover pieces too small to fit the cutter, she shapes the dough into a miniature version of the steel star in her hands. Once the biscuits are out of the oven, she lathers on lotion, feeling its cool, allowing it to soak in.

Palate: The beer on her husband's lips makes a perfume, blending with the camellia on her neck. Each night he comes in, sneaks behind her and kisses her. She stands at the stove with her back to him, the wire wool of his palms on her back sanding off her cold shoulders. The air is full of lemonade. She makes it cloudier than the air over the hills, serving it with a smile sharp as a lemon wedge. The kitchen is spotless. The plastic pots all sit inside one another on the shelf. Everything's as it should be. It's difficult for her to explain why the Tupperware matters to her so much, but it does. There's perhaps only one woman who could understand, her pen pal in Florida. Caroline shipped a sample and Bunny became hooked. The plastic pots were so wonderful to her she wanted to enlighten everyone. It felt good to share; she wondered what else was out there to save people time. Slicers, dicers, peelers and grinders, she'd discover them all. Some raise large families, some invent the light bulb, some paint the Sistine Chapel. Bunny Johnson leaves her legacy in every kitchen drawer for a mile. 'If it wasn't for me,' she says, 'the whole island would still be slicing their eggs wonky and no one's sandwich would last a day.'

Finish: She doesn't look unlike the Bunny Tyler she was, other than her aprons and the colour of her clothes. Gone are the Easter colours, in favour of magnolia, mushroom, mink, shades she feels are more fitting for a woman her age. She pauses when she says, 'a woman my age', waiting for someone to tell her she hasn't aged a day. Her aprons are crisp flags of colour in her pantry. They offer little protection from splashes and spills, anywhere but over her hips. Bunny knows this, yet she refuses to serve a meal without one, in it she is a wife wrapped in a bow.

Overall: She isn't so dissimilar to the woman her husband proposed to, but for the rules she lays down for her daughter, stiffer than the starch she irons into his shirts. The more the girl grows, the more starch Bunny uses. Sylvie's blouses don't move. Seth jokes Bunny uses so much starch the whole family wear shirts that resemble cardboard boxes with people inside.

It could be worse. Some men fell in love with beauty pageant contestants who let themselves go. Some married solid women who upped and died. Whenever Bunny corrected Sylvie, forced him go to church or griped about gambling, Seth remembered such facts. It really could be a lot worse. It wasn't his place to criticise the way she brought up her daughter – what did he know about girls?

The customers glared at the box Bunny plonked on the counter. It wasn't plastic but a rusty old biscuit tin with a hole in the lid. Where the label was, Bunny had stuck a square of brown paper and written 'SWEAR BOX'.

'I've been thinking, if you gentlemen are going to stand around using language that would put a sailor to shame, something positive may as well come of it,' Bunny said. 'Every time you swear, drop a coin in the box. The proceeds will go to the church's charitable fund.'

The men glanced at the tin. It didn't look big enough to fit in all their shits and fucks. There wasn't a large enough box in the world.

'I'll see you later.' Bunny pecked Seth's cheek. 'I may be a little late.'

Not many things stopped Bunny serving dinner at six on the dot: church, kitchenware saleswoman responsibilities, and meetings with TIM. TIM was short for The Island Mothers. There were several women in the group who didn't care for the acronym. The word reminded them of a kid who used to pick his nose. It was the name of an annoying brother. Or that dirty dog they once loved as a child, until it started to hump their favourite teddy bears. There were often furious debates about finding another name, but no one could agree on one.

The women continued to meet in the church hall and complain about what the kids were wearing these days, their loitering after school, and the records they swivelled their pelvises to. Lately, Sylvie and I could barely figure out how to dance to a song before it disappeared from the jukebox in the harbour café. The owner would apologise and give us the single without a plastic centre to take away.

'I'm sorry,' Harvey would say, smoothing his moustache, pale as milk foam. In summer, he left the café in the care of his wife to drive a van around the island selling ice cream. In winter, he got out the same van and did the rounds selling potatoes and tins of corned beef to anyone under the weather. He always waited in the lane, giving anyone the chance to scuttle for pennies, playing the same sunny tune regardless of what he had on board. In December, we'd hear him delivering sprouts and remember moving lighter than flowers in our breezy summer skirts. We'd lift our faces to receive the sunlight, forgetting, for a second, we were wearing so many woollies we could barely move our arms.

'Elvis has left the island,' Harvey once said, 'and he's taken Buddy Holly with him and all. Someone from The Island Mothers complained he was making her son walk too cocky. The last thing I want is those lot around here. Anything for a quiet life.' Sylvie had sighed and hummed the chorus of 'It's Now or Never'. Whenever a record disappeared, we'd spend the week humming it, singing the odd line we could remember out over the waves, until the song faded into another tune.

The air clung to Bunny's perfume long after she left the hardware store. The men lowered their voices. The swear box was a spy, listening to their every word.

'Let's get this straight, if I curse I'm supposed to drop a coin in the box and the money goes to the church?'

'That's right,' said Seth.

'What do they use it for?'

'I don't know, repairs and that. The church hall needs sprucing up a bit.'

'Who does the jobs?'

Seth polished a speck of wire wool off the counter with his cuff. 'I do, if I can. It's cheaper.'

The men laughed.

'Hold on, so the more I swear, the more they can afford to fix the place up. The busier you are on weekends! That wife of yours! She's got you where she wants you alright!'

Someone made a whipping sound with his tongue. The men laughed.

'Don't they all?' Seth laughed, but he looked relieved when they changed the subject to complain about their own wives. The flipping colour charts, the furniture, the rooms that had to be decorated to match their moods.

'Fifteen yellows the missus showed me. I painted a whole wall Buttercup and she said it didn't look like she imagined. What did she imagine? She said she preferred Primrose.' One man said. 'Looked the same to me. Yellow is yellow.'

On the other side of the store, Zach shook his head, listening without comment. For him, yellow was not yellow. He could give a woman Primrose, Buttercup, Sunflower, Honey, Autumn Rose, more yellows than anyone could dream of. I opened my purse and carried my brass hook to the till. Seth folded it into a paper bag and rang it up.

'Women are good for business,' he said. 'I can't complain.'

He honoured the right of his customers to figure out the mysteries of marriage with mutters and rants. It was his job to listen with a sympathetic nod of his head, but no one ever heard him complain about Bunny, no matter what she did.

There's a skein of geese winging over when I spot the fella out the window. Beard like a crow's nest clagged in hoar frost. It's that wild and white. He opens Lorrie's gate, drags something out of a sack under his arm and lays it on the step. It's so early no one's awake but me and the birds. The milk bottles are studded in dew and coal tits peck at the foil. The curtains are closed. Everyone's in their beds but me and the old fella.

I got up because of this dream I had. I was kissing some lad I couldn't see. I could feel hands all over me dragging me into the sea.

I watch, but can't make out what the stranger's leaving next door. It looks soft and flecked in the not-quite-morning light. He wipes his hands on his jeans, nicks a pint of milk off the step and scuttles up the path.

I'm all set to ask Lorrie about it, but I forget when she comes over. I forget about everything but Ma sniffing about in the hall. Cuddling a stack of laundry and pressing her ear to the door. Lorrie's flicking through this catalogue. We're playing this game we've been playing forever. The rule is we have to pick our future off whatever page we turn. Or else. We lay on our bellies with our chins on our fists. Laughing like philosophers who've been at the laughing gas.

'I want that oven, but in that kitchen. I want that kettle. Dibs.' Lorrie points at the page. And I've got to pick something fast. Or get stuck with the leftovers. I can't choose the same stuff as Lorrie. It's THE LAW. No self-respecting lassie would have the same sofa as the woman next door. Not even if it's only in a house in her head.

Once our fictional houses are furnished, we start looking for a fella. It's dead easy to find one. They're all in menswear. Just hanging about in cardigans. Staring at their watches. Waiting to be picked. Some are wearing caps, and some have wallets. There's a fair few looking into the distance like they can sorta see us getting off a boat and tottering into their arms. We're so late. Some of them are so sick of waiting they'll be off any minute. They'll be skiving off to the pub to get plastered I reckon. They have that look.

'Who would you marry off this page?' Lorrie says. 'This guy? He looks handy with a fishing rod. Look at that tackle.'

She flicks the page. It's all vests and skids. Spidery-looking hair crawling out of their vests. Their undies look like they've got a bunch of keys in there, a Fry's Chocolate Cream, a bag of marbles and a shitload of other stuff they're storing for later. Maybe that's why fellas don't need handbags.

'What's that?' My finger slides along the page. 'This lad looks like he's carrying a sack of tatties between his legs.'

Lorrie laughs. 'He might be.'

It's stotting down out. The rain pitter-patters all around the house and gives Ma the excuse to come in she's been desperate for. Cocoa's her ruse. She sets a cup down and hovers about like she wants to kick about in my room and remember being a young lass for a bit.

'What are you girls up to?' She peers over our shoulders.

'Nothing,' Lorrie says. 'Sylvie was just saying she wants to marry a fisherman.'

'No I wasn't!'

I clout Lorrie with a cushion. We've both got the giggles.

The giggles won't stop. They feel like a ladder in a stocking, running away from the wee nick that set them off.

'Don't set your hearts on anything, girls. You don't have to marry anyone if you don't want to. Actually, I think Sylvie would suit being a nun,' Ma says, casual as some women say their daughters should wear blue to match their eyes or something.

She beams and pops her head around the door before she goes. 'Don't let your cocoa go cold, girls. Look, it's already getting a skin.'

'Nun!'

Lorrie drags my cardigan over my head like a woolly wimple. I smile, but the giggles have scarpered. I suddenly remember who I am.

'Hmm.'

Ma waves at Lorrie on her way out. She's crossing the path with a borrowed umbrella and a skirt that makes her wiggle.

'I'm not sure about your pal lately,' Ma says as we turn to come in. 'She's a bad influence, I think.'

'We were just mucking around. It didn't mean anything.'

'Hmm,' she says again.

I wonder what the 'hmm' means. Hmm always means something. Hmm can mean ten thousand things when she says it. And none of them are good.

LORRIE

Sylvie dropped Johnny Cash on the portable record player Seth gave her for her birthday. It had belonged to a customer struggling to pay his bills. Though he hadn't been considering buying one, the man brought it into the store and Seth thought of Sylvie. It resembled a vanity case. Pretty. Ivory leatherette. Gold dials. He shook the farmer's hand and promised to wipe his slate clean. Sure, he'd be happy to take it; his daughter would love it. The farmer wiped his face, trying not to think of the faces of his children when he took it away.

I stared at the door. Zach's room was across the landing. No more than a door, a hall, and another door separated me from him lying on his bed, listening to the woodpecker outside Sylvie kept talking about, combing Brylcreem into his hair, and unbuttoning his work shirt with his name embroidered on his chest. I dawdled my way to the bathroom and pictured bumping into him. He'd see me in angora. I'd bump into him so hard he'd almost fall. It would change everything. I'd smile in one of a hundred ways I'd practised in the mirror. He'd look at me and realise he'd never really seen me before. He wouldn't see me as some kid his stepsister knew. He'd finally see me as a girl and fall for me. I lingered by his door for as long possible, but nothing stirred.

'What's Zach like when he's not at work?' I asked.

Sylvie flicked shut a magazine and crumpled something she'd ripped out of it up the sleeve of her cardigan. I recalled her outside in her pyjamas, scrabbling through paper, looking so ashamed my mother felt it would be cruel for me to mention it and embarrass her.

'What's that?' I tugged her cardigan and the bit of paper fell to the floor. It was a photo of a man and a woman kissing in the rain. There were puddles of street light everywhere.

'Nothing.' Sylvie snatched the picture away. 'You're always going on about Zach!' she said. 'Change the record. He's not that interesting.'

The boy was furniture to her, a stepbrother there at dinner alongside the pepper, a figure in front of the TV with a foot on the pouf blocking her view. Every now and then, they swapped the furniture in their bedrooms or traded a watch for a mechanical pencil, but they never killed time together.

'What's he really like?' I wanted to know.

'I don't know. He's not exactly a chatterbox. He doesn't haver on. He can stay in the bath so long I had to wee in a bucket once. Oh, and he eats cereal without getting out a bowl.'

When I got married, I decided I'd want it to be to someone who ate his cereal without dirtying a bowl. It was thoughtful. Fewer dishes to wash, more time to love.

'What does he talk about?'

'Fishing. Paint. The importance of undercoat.'

It was frustrating, chatting to Sylvie about the opposite sex. Not just Zach, anyone. I was only a month older than her, but it seemed a decade. Poring through my magazine full of singers and actors with doe eyes, she nibbled a Tunnock's wafer without a glance.

'Who do you fancy?' I asked.

'No one.'

'Come on, you must like someone.'

'Why do I have to?'

I didn't answer, I supposed she had to have a crush on someone because I did. I wanted the company.

'What about Frank Sinatra?' I asked. 'Do you like him?'

Sylvie folded the biscuit wrapper, thinking.

'I don't mind his songs. I like his eyes, there's something mean about him though. He looks like he can smell something bad. Look at him' – she held up a magazine – 'he looks like he's staring at you and accusing you of farting.'

'What about Elvis then? Don't you think he's handsome?'

'Yeah, but' – Sylvie got up to get her satchel off the hook – 'I dunno, his mouth has a look to it like someone just whispered something dead sad to him and he's trying not to bawl his eyes out. Have you done your English assignment?' she asked. 'Do you want to start?'

'Not particularly. There's plenty of time.'

Sylvie sharpened a pencil. She wouldn't just do one assignment, she'd start more than one if she could. It was the way she'd always been. Even in the juniors, when she was off school sick, the teacher sometimes sent her strange topics to write essays about 'just for fun'. I'd never understand it.

I slipped on my shoes. If Sylvie was going to be boring, I'd rather go. My father was at work, and if I caught my mother at the right time, I could ask for a raise in my pocket money. I wanted it so much I'd even do ironing. I saw Rook Cutler's van outside and grinned. I wouldn't need to make any promises I didn't intend to keep. Everything would be fine. When Rook was around, it was always the right time.

Rook lay on the floor gazing at the pipes under the sink. He had come to replace every pipe in the house not long after we moved in. Ever since, my mother called him whenever something needed to be fixed.

'The sink's blocked again,' she said.

Rook looked up, his dark hair in his eyes. There was a custom in his family of naming babies after wild things, Roses, Violets, Heathers and Ferns. His mother was surrounded by so many flowers as a child she vowed to be different when the time came. Wren, Robin, Dove and Rook, she named all her children after birds. Rook was the last. He suited his name.

'Pass me the wrench. No, that one there,' he said.

She held out the silver metal. His fingers curled around the handle. She let go. They didn't touch, but it gave the impression they did. It created the same impression as when I would come in and she'd bustle off to wash the coffee cups, or brush crumbs off a plate, clearing away their laughter before anyone saw.

'There you go.' Rook pulled a wad of butter out of the bend. It had melted and set into a U shape. The pair laughed. It was a different laugh to the one she usually had. It made it seem a laugh is a wild thing that becomes tamed by years. Every year, my mother's laugh took up less space in the room, other than when Rook was around. This was the laugh she'd had when she was young, or as near to it as she could find.

AN EVALUATION OF ROOK CUTLER

Nose: A rub of rust from the handle of his ancient toolbox freckles his fingers, hints of the leaves he lets blow into his open car window catch in his hair. He never closes it, not even in winter. He always smells of work and bits of woodland caught in his pockets. He allows it to stay there for as long as it will.

Palate: Coffee, the trout he catches every season, oak and treacle from the whisky he sniffs on bottling days. My grandfather has been hiring him on a casual basis for years, the rest of the time he's a plumber, fixing cisterns in windy outhouses, and fitting aspirational bathrooms indoors. When business is good, he closes his eyes and lifts a glass in the distillery doorway, allowing the sun to linger on his face as the amber slides down.

Finish: There's a glow to his skin. It's more olive than most people on the island, who are so pale it's possible to the see the veins in their arms, the colour of Stilton. He glows with a sheen of work, the heat of the distillery and the graft of fitting pipes. On fine days, sitting with my mother outside, his hazel eyes are fires that won't die. His is a neck that has never graced a tie, something about this small fact seems to show on his face.

Overall: The man my mother knew as a child playing Cowboys and Indians. The pair of them still occasionally look like they remember those days, and, that if they weren't supposed to be adults, they could both start playing again at any time.

Rook refused to call my mother by her Christian name, unlike my father: 'Cora, will you be careful with your chequebook next time? . . . I don't know, Cora, I shouldn't have listened to you. I should have been doing my job . . . I don't think we should fit a bathroom yet, Cora. I know it's Baltic in the outhouse, but I'm sick of having workmen around. I'm sorely tempted to have a go myself.'

Rook addressed my mother with the nickname she'd had as a child, born of a narrow escape from a wild goat and her talent for finding pennies on the ground. I'd never heard her speak of him before we came to the island and I found their photo under the floor in my room. On the back, she had written *Cora & Rook*, drawn a heart, then scribbled it out. It seemed he simply walked into our lives one day with a wrench, wiped his feet at the door, and made my mother someone else.

'Lucky?' he said.

'Rook, long time no . . . '

The smile she gave him was a hundred miles away from her Yes Dear and That's Nice smiles. It shone sharper than flint skimming water. It splashed light into her eyes.

Rook wiped his hands on a cloth, closed the cupboard under the sink, and took the beer she'd now handed him. It was still light outside, an unusually warm breeze shivered across the island, supper was already prepared, her work was done.

'Let's sit outside and watch the sun come around,' she said.

There was an hour when the sun hit the tin roof of the barn and made it an object of beauty. Rook and my mother sat on adjacent deckchairs sipping beers. I listened to their voices rise and fall through the open window, fascinated. They never spoke about anything but the weather, Grumps, whisky and plumbing, not that I'd heard, yet somehow their voices found a way to make the mundane sound fragile and personal.

'I try to have one spontaneous moment a day,' she said. 'A minute or so just for me: a beer, a slither of a sunset, a moment doing absolutely nothing but watching the grass grow.'

'It's not spontaneous if you plan it,' said Rook.

'You're right there.' She laughed. 'I don't get to be spontaneous these days unless I put it on my list of Things to Do Today.'

'You're an amazing woman,' he said.

'You're an amazing . . . you're not so bad yourself.'

'An amazing what?'

Rook slicked a hand over his fringe without caring that it never stayed put. I saw why someone might want to sit with him for a while. Some people are so comfortable in their own skin, it rubs off.

'I'm still deciding what you are,' she laughed. 'I don't think I'll ever know. I'll go with friend.'

'I'll take that.' They chinked their bottles and swigged.

'Do you remember that crow we found? Right over there . . . '

Rook pointed to the whisky sheds, the site of their childhood hide-and-seek games.

'That fledgling! Mr Bollocks. That's what Pa called him. He was so loud. Talking bollocks from dusk till dawn, Pa said. Oh, yes! I loved that bird. I wanted it to learn to say my name!' She laughed, a girl with a crow on her shoulder he watched fly away.

The gravel further along the lane crunched softly, dust and small stones being disturbed. She recognised my father's footsteps before he turned past the rosehips and came into sight. His walk always gave the impression he was carrying along something heavy.

'Well, I'd better get moving . . . '

She swigged the last of her drink and clinked the bottles into the box to take back to the shop. Lucky no more, at least not until Rook returned.

THE COLLECTOR OF KISSES – A PAPER ON HOBBIES

There's not a name for my hobby, like crochet, quilting or knitting. It's not useful. Loads of hobbies are better than mine. Some lassies cross-stitch cases for their grandmas' specs, some knit their brothers a scarf that trails on the ground. Others carry sketch books wherever they go. I've seen lassies like that fall over, stand up and look for somewhere to sit. They flip open a page and sketch a bird with feathers so fine it could fly off the page and carry all their clumsiness away. I'm dead jealous of folks like that. Lassies who make pictures that can be put on a wall. I keep my hobby a secret, even from Ma. Especially from her. She must never know.

I carry a scalpel in my pocket wherever I go kinda like an artist clutches a pencil to feel whole. I stroke its steel handle and wait for a chance to slice my hobby into my day. I offer to carry out the rubbish. And when I'm outside, I kneel on the floor and flick, flick, flick through papers and old magazines. I'm on the lookout for stuff for my scrapbook. When I find the right picture, I cut it out. I keep my eyes peeled at the dentists and doctors, on buses and on benches. I look out for the magazines the lady next door is done with. Lately, since this one time she caught me going through her magazines, she never puts them in the bin any more. Instead, she leaves them stacked next to it like someone leaving a bowl of milk out for a cat. I'm glad. It saves me riffling through leftovers and soggy tea leaves for a photo of Scarlett O'Hara bending over backwards. Or Marilyn Monroe blowing a soft dove-grey kiss.

I don't care that much about the films they were in. Films never seem to have much to do with me. They're all in places where it's always July and all the folks have shiny teeth so flat I bet they never ate meat, or had to bite anyone, their whole life. What I care about is what they're doing with their lips. I collect pictures of kisses like stamps. They are stamps, I think, a kiss is a stamp of approval folks stick all over.

I study the pictures like wee lads pick up insects, because I want to understand how they work. The photos make kissing look dead easy. Simple as learning to swim. Step One: Close your eyes. Step Two: Lean in. Step Three: Pucker up. Give in. Let go of the daylight, the stars, the moon.

The kisses in my book are bonnie things. None of them make me fearty. In my scrapbook a kiss is just a kiss.

Each night, I've got to wait until Ma stops clickety-clicking about in her slippers. Then I climb out of bed and drag my collection out from under the dresser. I flick on a torch and stare at the pictures like a lesson I can learn. I snuggle up under the covers counting kisses instead of sheep. There's not a day I don't look for more pictures. Some hobbies are that way, I reckon. Even when you want to be away they won't let you be. They follow you about the place, watching and waiting. Wanting a wee bit more of your day. I don't know when a hobby becomes an obsession. I reckon when it feels so normal it's like breathing. That's what my hobby is, something like breathing. When I see lassies my age kissing their boyfriends without a care in the world I look around for dropped magazines with something inside I can take away. This way I can breathe.

I read through my work and rip the page out of my notebook. Then I rip the pages into bits small as snowflakes, just to be sure. I swallow a deep breath and start all over again:

A PAPER ON HOBBIES, WHY I LOVE CROSS-STITCH

I love to cross-stitch. I love the silks and the feel of all the colours in my hands. I can't do all the stitches, but I can unpick all my mistakes and start over with a shiny new thread.

It's all a pile of shite. Every word I write is bollocks. Just like it should be. Ma would be proud.

LORRIE

There was sleet over Easter. Once it had cleared, we charged out of the house and ruined my parents' marriage. Or perhaps we didn't, and something had been wrong for a while and the only thing that really changed was me. I could suddenly see it.

It was an ordinary morning. Grumps shovelled a dead barn owl off the distillery steps and waved as we drove along the lane. It was rare for my father to be off work at the same time we weren't at school. My mother packed a picnic and we crammed into the car, bored with being told to keep it down over the holidays: 'Your father has a headache . . . Your father is reading the paper. Can't you see he's trying to concentrate? He needs to relax. You aren't helping.' Honestly, I don't think we ever saw him completely relaxed. Relaxation was an alien concept. Even lounging in his favourite chair, he would run his thumb over his teeth constantly, never completely at ease, whittling a fingernail down to a stump.

Toby sat in the back seat next to me doing tricks with string. I sang 'I Walk the Line' to myself, though it wasn't on the radio. My mother read all the road signs out loud.

'I like the deer sign,' she said. 'It's my favourite. It always cheers up the road even if you never see a deer.'

The sun was out, though the air was sharp. Families seized their chance to dip their toes in the lake and dragged out rowing boats. My mother rolled out a tartan blanket and set the picnic basket down. I stripped down to the bathing suit I'd snuck on under my clothes and stood on the shingle beach anticipating the shock of the cold, the shiver putting my feet in the water would ripple down my spine.

'Cora,' my father said, 'we have to go. Now.'

He looked as if he'd been running, the colour flaring high in his cheeks. My mother looked confused. The bread was already buttered. The plates were all set out on the blanket. The ants were eyeing up the biscuits.

'What are you talking about? We've just got here, we haven't even had lunch.'

'I've just seen Tony Fletcher.'

My father looked towards a lone orange dinghy drifting out over the water.

'Whatever's he doing here? He's a long way from home.'

'I don't know, Cora. And I don't care. Pack up our stuff. I'll wait in the car.'

We trudged over the shale with beach towels rolled under our arms while my father waited with his keys in the ignition, fingers tapping the wheel.

AN EVALUATION OF TONY FLETCHER

Nose: Bread, baby powder, and the coal-tar soap his wife is convinced will help the eczema that flares up on one side of his face, baked by the shop window all summer. He is a man made of his work. Even on Sundays he smells of bread. If you cut him he'd bleed puffs of flour.

Palate: The sugar glaze he stirs in a cup for his famous sweet rolls, a dash of cinnamon sprinkled on top, he dips a wooden spoon in and sucks it before he washes his hands. There's a splash of vinegar on his tongue from the salad his wife insists on bringing him at lunchtime, patting his belly, not as flat as it was, swollen with family life. What can he say? He must sample his wares. His wife can cook. He never saw a skinny guy who looked loved.

Finish: There's a cloud of flour that follows him wherever he goes. Even in his Sunday clothes, he'd sometimes find patches of white on his sleeves. Unhooking a dry-cleaning bag from a shelf behind the bakery, he put on the black suit a week after the fire and sighed, brushing off flour, resigned to imperfect trousers as his mother-in-law's coffin was lowered into the ground.

Overall: A man who knows how to shrug and say, 'These things happen, we're lucky, we're still here' as he sets up a foldaway bed in the stockroom behind the bakery. The night following the accident, he began dreaming of dough rising and would wake up with a hankering to add rosemary, cheese, or onions to various loaves he'd call Loaf of the Day. He'd display these in the shop window and put out a chalkboard. Writing the name of the bread in green chalk, he'd smile, certain he'd be back on his feet in no time at all.

It was a beautiful day, the last time we ever bought a loaf from Fletcher's. We weren't even considering moving to the island then. My mother was loving the sun. She put down the paring knife, let the apples brown and leapt on my father as soon as he came in. The summer brought out another side of her. She was hankering for one of her spontaneous hours. Right now.

'Let's go for a stroll by the pier. I've been chained to the kitchen all day. We'll axe dinner and pick up something while we're out.'

'I have to go to the office for some documents,' my father replied. 'Can you believe Tony Fletcher has no insurance on his house? Never has done. He hates forms, that was his excuse! The papers are ready. I just have to get his signature.'

She sighed, interested in listening to nothing but penny slot machines and the waves washing up mussel shells.

'Come on, it's lovely out! You can do it tomorrow. He won't mind.'

'Pleeeeease come with us,' Toby whined. He hadn't been in school long and considered it an affront to his free time. 'You're never here while it's still light.'

My father didn't have the energy to argue with us all. We bought ice cream and strolled by the sun-bleached pier watching women in blustery skirts drop coins into telescopes to stare at the gulls coasting in. I flicked an insect away from my raspberry ripple and saw Toby raise a slow hand to his ear. The wasp hovered and flew on.

'What the . . . ?'

Mum stared at Toby, wide-eyed, his ear going purple, swelling faster than a finger jammed in a door. He didn't cry. The look on his face reminded me of a boxer who didn't know he'd been knocked out yet, but it couldn't be long until he'd fall to the floor.

'He's been stung! Do something.'

At around the time the baker would have been inviting my father in and offering him a bag of Eccles cakes to give to the kids, we were driving to Casualty, filling in forms about allergies and gripping Toby's knuckles as the needle loomed towards him to bring the swelling down.

'It's too late to do anything now.' My mother leant against my father's shoulder, exhausted. Toby leant against her leg, rubbing one bandaged ear, a strip of gauze surrounding his chubby face to hold it in place.

'The baby will be asleep,' my father said. 'I'll go in the morning.'

The fire started after midnight. One of the cigarettes the baker's mother-in-law couldn't light without saying 'I really should quit' had smouldered in an ashtray in the attic. The woman always hated that bedroom. It was draughty. The ceiling sloped. But she claimed she'd rather crouch than suffer her son-in-law's snoring she insisted she could hear in every other inch of the house.

The house didn't burn to the ground. It might have been better for my father if it had. Every day we had to walk past the blackened walls and absent roof, its charcoal trusses framing the clouds. 'Look on the bright side, at least Tony and his wife got out with the baby,' my mother had said, 'and he still has the bakery.' 'He should have been insured. He should have done it years ago!' My father called Tony a fool, but blamed himself. He believed if he hadn't gone for a stroll, if his wife hadn't suggested it, if it wasn't for ice cream and wasps, if, if, if . . . Tony and his family wouldn't be resting their heads on bags of flour. 'That's the last time I'm listening to you and your flights of fancy,' he'd said.

I never saw my mother attempt to include him in one of her spontaneous moments after that. She kept them reserved for giving sudden choc ices to me and my brother, letting me cut her fringe in the kitchen because she fancied a change, sitting in a deckchair at noon for ten minutes, and for Rook Cutler, doing nothing with him but being herself.

The silence stifled us on the journey from the lake. I suddenly missed the coast where we used to live, the swirl of the roller coaster, the bustling crowds on the pier. It was always loud enough to lose yourself in. Here, the irritation of the adults pressed in closer than the storm we could see gathering over the hills.

'Thinking about it, his wife had family on the island. Cousins, I think. I was chatting to her about it once,' my mother said. 'I suppose that's why they're here. It's a small world.'

'I don't care.' My father kept his eyes on the road.

'It wasn't your fault, you know. You did all you could to help them. You put your job on the line. Things happen. You can't be responsible for everything.'

'It beats not being responsible for anything.'

They didn't speak after that. She twisted in her seat, focusing on Toby and his illusion of 'unsnapped' string.

'Well done. You're getting better. You'll be like Houdini one day.'

'I don't want to be like Houdini. I want to be like me,' Toby said.

I stared at the back of my father's head, the knots in his neck. No day out with him was ever much fun. Wherever he took us, he was constantly reminding us to keep our voices down, watch where we were standing, and mind our manners. He seemed to shoulder the responsibility for anything his life happened to brush by. It made it difficult to show him any sort of affection – caution held us back. Yet I almost wanted to hug him when we piled into the car. He stared out of the window, chewing his lip, watching a plump man splashing his wife and son on the shore. I had never seen anyone look so alone. Even when my mother slammed the picnic hamper into the boot, and Toby dangled a yo-yo out of the window, scraping the passenger door, my father didn't seem to hear it. Whatever he was thinking was louder than us all.

It's crazy when I'm bored I'm sorta off my head. It can happen in a flash. *Boom!* This itchiness creeps over my hands and I can't stop them fiddling and being daft. I'll do something pointless, like stick my lip in a pop bottle and suck it just to feel it latch on like a leech. Or I'll grab a wee bit of string and wind it around my finger. Round and round, just to see how blue my pinkie can get. I'll shove a flower in my mouth even though Lorrie's there.

I have these daffodils in the blue jug by my bed. Just a few, hanging their heads and feeling sorry for themselves. I pick one up while Lorrie's raking through my wardrobe. Fidgety, I dust the petals over my chin and pop the whole thing in my mouth. Just like that. I stick it in the water again.

'How did you do that?'

Lorrie's holding a coat hanger. There's nothing I've got she wants to borrow.

'I didn't do nowt,' I say.

Shite. I didn't know she was looking. I wasn't thinking, at least my fidgety fingers weren't.

Lorrie comes closer, eyeing the rose. My least favourite dress hangs in her hand. Swaying like it fancies a dance.

'You did! You swapped the flower for a fresh one. It looks different. Show me how you did it! I'd love to know a trick Toby doesn't know. It'll drive him up the wall.'

'That would be telling.'

I'm trying to sound mysterious, like a magician who never reveals his tricks. I'm not sure I pull it off though. I'm going beetroot. Panicking a bit. It's alright. Lorrie's already returned to the wardrobe. It's a lost cause.

'It's hopeless. You officially have no clothes that don't belong on a Sunday-school teacher.'

She clatters her bag onto the patchwork bedspread and comes at me with the eye pencil.

'Let me do something to bring your eyes out at least. Look, like this.'

I let her 'bring my eyes out', even though it sounds like a crazy scientist collecting body parts to make Frankenstein a missus. Ma might come in any second. I can hear her downstairs chopping potatoes, clunking them into the pan. The knife stops chopping. I freeze.

'That's enough now, Ma might come in,' I say.

'Come on! It's fun.' Lorrie's voice dips. 'It's not like your mother doesn't doll herself up. That make-up isn't as invisible as she thinks.'

I smack away Lorrie's hand before the eyeliner touches my face.

'Don't you want to look pretty?' she asks.

'Not really,' I say. 'What good would it do anyone?'

'You could catch someone's eye, someone nice, if you tried. Someone might even ask you to the dance.'

I pick up another daffodil, hold it to my nose and sniff. Just to stop myself running it over my lips. There's no way I'm going to admit I've already caught someone's eye. Someone nice. Lorrie doesn't know squat about the note I got in class. If I tell her, I'll never hear the last of it. Sylvie & Joe, sitting in a tree, K I S S I N G . . . I won't be telling her nothing. She'd go doolally.

LORRIE

Joe Clark was staring at me. He had to be. Sylvie was the only other person around, and she'd never worn anything uglier. Bunny had waved us on our way that morning and I'd handed Sylvie my lipstick as soon as we were out of sight: 'I don't want it.' Sylvie had stormed along the lane, plain as day. Plainer. It was spring. The air buzzed with the rumour of summer on its way. Sylvie shuffled along in a long skirt and cardigan Bunny had knitted, browner than the path under our feet.

Joe stood opposite the water fountain. I lowered my head and whispered to Sylvie, 'Is it just me, or is he looking over?'

Sylvie bent to the water.

'He's looking at you!' I said.

I may have sounded jealous, because I was. Of all the people for the boy to notice, it shouldn't have been Sylvie. I didn't think of it as being catty. It was a fact as simple to me as people maths: *Shy girl without lipstick + dress sized up from the pattern of a pinafore she wore when she was seven + cute boy ÷ the sort of girls who do gymnastics after school, dancing around him all day, dragging him into any conversation, queuing to sign their name on the cast on his arm = This Boy can do Better than this Girl.*

Joe's arm was covered in a cast to his elbow. The plaster was covered in doodles of stickmen and the names of girls he had to carry around for six weeks. He came towards us scratching it with a pencil. Sylvie wiped her chin with her sleeve.

'I was wondering if you fancy going out sometime, Sylvie?' he asked. 'Maybe up to the lighthouse to see the puffins or something?'

He sounded afraid to make a sound that might scare a wild bird away. I waited for Sylvie to clam up or stutter, the way she did when she had to read aloud in class. But she didn't.

'What for?' she said. 'Why would you want me to go?'

'I dunno, just for the company.'

'I don't think so.' Sylvie charged down the corridor and turned back, calling, 'Learn to love your own company.'

I chased after her.

'That was so rude. Joe Clark! He's so sweet,' I said. 'Why would you turn him down?'

I recalled one of my grandfather's favourite expressions: 'If someone gives you the moon on a stick, you have to be bright enough to lick it.'

'You have the moon,' Sylvie said. 'I don't give a shite.'

I gasped. Sylvie never swore. She licked her lips after she spoke, tasting something she'd never tried before but could get used to.

'You should go out with him. Just look at him,' I said.

'I've seen him. I've seen more than I want.'

It never occurred to me Sylvie could get angry. I saw her be shy, mumble and stare into space sometimes, but she didn't get angry. It occurred to me that perhaps she did, but didn't really know how to show it. She popped a sour plum in her mouth and bit it with a crack. I reeled off a list of girls who'd kill to go out with Joe, selling him to her.

'You don't know how lucky you are,' I said.

'I'm not lucky. You go out with him, if you like him so much. I don't want to. I'm not you. Stop telling me I have to be.'

She stormed into the Domestic Science room without looking back.

We didn't speak on the way home, but it couldn't last. The silence between my parents was palpable over dinner. There had been a stiff-lipped sort of courtesy between them ever since the lake. I overheard the odd word, and understood my father had lost his job in insurance after altering the date on a form, but I never heard my mother blame him. Rather, the whole incident confirmed they were so different that each day together was a chore. They refused to argue in our presence, instead they were painfully polite.

My mother placed a drink on a coaster and my father said thanks. He stacked the plates for her, and she expressed her gratitude. Other than that, their only conversations involved Toby showing us card tricks.

'You're better off practising long division, son,' my father said. 'Something useful. One day you'll wake up an adult and won't even remember whatever it was you used to want to be.'

'It's a wonderful trick,' Mum said. 'Let him dream while he can.'

The silence resumed and my parents returned to reminding me of performers in a play, wandering through rooms, shuffling props, knowing they were supposed to be man and wife. Their politeness was a mask, underneath no one was smiling. The string was about to snap. I did the dishes, left them on the drying rack and ducked out to Sylvie's before the water had drained from the sink.

'What a jolly-looking skirt! It's so snug! Well, I suppose a windy day won't bother it!'

Bunny commented on my outfit as soon as she saw me. I smiled and complimented her apron, willing to swallow more of her gingerbread than I could stand rather than be in the house at the same time as my parents.

I can kinda feel it coming like you can feel snow before a single flake falls. That crackling in the air brittle with cold. The lad's staring at us and I just keep guzzling water slow as a cow. But inside I'm screaming. God, please don't come over. Please don't like me, especially in front of Lorrie. Jesus, she'll never understand.

I press the knob on the fountain and fill my gob with lukewarm water. Then, he's right here. And I all I can think of is callipers and orange ice lollies melting in his ma's sticky hands. I look at the parquet floor and spot a button on the floor someone must have fidgeted off their coat. It's shiny red. And bigger than a farthing. I picture some lassie shivering in a coat that'll never fasten all the way up ever again.

Joe starts blethering. And I picture a wee lad. Big lads racing past him with a ball. I see him clutching the guitar his ma got him for Christmas. I gobble more water, wanting to wash the memory out of my gob.

I reject him like pulling off a plaster. *Zap!* Quick as I can. I rush away from the sting. I swear not to look back. I won't look. I won't meet his eye. I just won't. I won't start blubbering in front of him.

The satchel honks of leather when I take out the note. How Joe gave me it goes like this: I'm just minding my own business in Biology. The frogs are all laid out on the desks. And

Joe wanders by, drops the note and scurries off to his stool. I pick it up before anyone sees it. Quick, if I'm fast enough it never happened and I won't have to look at it. Joe picks up a frog at his workbench and lets its legs jiggle, dancing a funny wee dead dance. I unfold the note. *Do you want to go to out with me some time, Sylvie? x*

Bollocks. What did he have to go and ask me that for? I shake my head. No, and I'm pretty sure 'sometime' is one word. I scrumple the note in my satchel and stare at my frog, gripping the scalpel. I'll not look at the lad. I have a frog to deal with. It died just for me to learn something. The skin makes a zipping sound under my blade. I dissect it like cutting off the bit of me that stings to have caused the look on Joe's face when he saw me crumple the note.

I stroke the inky kiss scratched after my name. There's a wee scribbly sketch of a scraggly flower on the corner of the paper. It's not drawn well enough for me to know what sort of flower it is, but if I hold it close to my face I can almost smell it. It smells of hope. Joe's hope I'll like him and we'll go see puffins and the sun will get out. And if it goes in, there'll be a flask of cocoa and I'll borrow his coat, if I'm cold. I'll snuggle into it like it's the lad's arms. I flatten the paper between the pages of a book and slip it onto the shelf alongside a pressed violet. I reckon it won't hurt. I like knowing it's there, I suppose.

The church hall groaned with the middle-aged men dragging the frame out of storage. Bunny followed everyone out and watched Seth screw wooden batons to the legs of a table.

'I'm still not sure we should have the stall this year,' she said.

Seth scratched his head, a fleck of coral paint sticking to his face.

'It's just a bit of fun! You never had a problem with it before. Besides, like you keep telling me about the swear box, it's all for a worthy cause.'

The fair was an annual event to raise funds for the Christmas lights fund, and the village flower displays (always, but always, overpopulated with marigolds and the foxgloves that popped up everywhere). People flocked to the field opposite the church to show off their chutney-making skills, sell bread and smoked fish, or to kiss someone on the lips. All for charity, of course.

The kissing booth was an institution. No one could remember how it began, but it had been going so long not even Bunny could stand in its way.

Bunny wandered away from her husband and set up her own stall, an arrangement of biscuits and cakes, fudge and tablet, wonder whisks, nesting bowls and the measuring scoops she used to bake. Everything was for sale. Wives wandered in with children in band uniforms cuddling bagpipes. The music billowed over laughter and chatter, flapping bunting fighting the wind. The fair was in full swing by lunchtime. The cake stall was open for business, and so was the Kissing Booth.

It was mostly husbands who gave the stall their patronage. One by one, they would pay their wives for a kiss they could get for taking out the rubbish or changing a light bulb. They'd stride up, clanking their coins into the pot, and make a song and dance about the amount. 'It was worth every penny,' one man would say, the same as the man before him. The women made how much their men paid a source of shy pride and dispute. 'That's all you gave me? You make me look a right woofer!' Husbands learnt to pay all they could, after years when the complaints of their wives had steamed up the car windows all the way home.

I saw my mother make her way to the stall. The pharmacist's wife was still in situ. Her husband fumbled for change as she bit into a pickled onion and lunged at him to kiss him with vinegar streaming down her chin. Everyone cheered. It had become a ritual with the pair, following a year they'd had a fight and she'd stuffed a fistful of wild garlic in her mouth out of spite. The laughter surrounding the couple made them forget they'd been arguing somehow. They couldn't help but join in. It had been pickled onion, anchovy and slippery garlic butter kisses all the way ever since. The worse the pickle, the greater the applause, the stronger their marriage.

'See you next year!'

The pharmacist's wife laughed and stepped around the stall, making way for her successor. My mother slipped behind the counter and waited for my father, who was showing Toby the proper way to Hook a Duck and taking his time to arrive. Rook Cutler wandered along with his hands in his pockets, uncertain what to do without a toolbox in his grip. It appeared he was considering giving the stall his business, but thought better of it. The rules weren't written down, but everyone knew:

1. No man could approach anyone else's wife. It simply wasn't done
2. No woman could be persuaded to man the booth, or rather, woman it, if she didn't want to
3. Anyone could take a break whenever they wanted, to dodge the horror of a forgotten sweetheart looming out of the past, or to avoid speaking to a husband who was in the doghouse for coming in off his face just last night
4. No girl under eighteen could work the stall, and no one with a cold or a split lip
5. The liberal use of mints and humbugs was encouraged

Rook wasn't a man to challenge the rules. He sidled over, keeping my mother company with small talk about the weather and some hiker who'd slipped on the hills.

'Lovely day, Lucky.'

The sun hung over them.

'It certainly is, Rook.' She looked up. 'It's a bonnie blue one.'

'OK, I'm here, I'm here.' My father nudged between them with his wallet. 'Let's get this over with, I haven't got all day . . . '

He placed down his money – not the most anyone had given their wives that day, and not the least. One hand on the counter, and one in his pocket, he leant towards his wife. She kissed him with her eyes open. Over his shoulder, I saw her gaze meet Rook Cutler's. He looked at her and looked down at his hands. It was a surrogate kiss. The first time my mother ever kissed her childhood sweetheart, she did so with her eyes while her husband's lips bore the weight. It didn't last long. The crowd shuffled in front of them, a large woman elbowing through it, complaining about the humidity, the midgies feasting on her arms, and everyone in her damn way. She waddled up to the booth, lifted her handbag upside down and let it rain coins all over the counter. They rattled and rolled everywhere.

'Count it, all of it,' she said, 'for your church, or whatever it is you do with it. It's all yours, if Sylvie Johnson will kiss my son.'

IF YOU COULD TRAVEL ANYWHERE IN TIME, WHERE WOULD YOU GO AND WHO WOULD YOU MEET?

I reckon I'm probably supposed to say something about history and show what I've learnt or something. I should tell you I want to go and advise Queen Victoria on how to get her head around grief. Or maybe go and be Hitler's babysitter or something, but I don't want to. The person I'd visit, if I could go anywhere, is Ma when I was a wee dot of a thing.

She'd be standing in the kitchen in a black dress. Chopping the crusts off sandwiches left over from my father's wake. She'd be worrying if we could get through all the leftovers before they went stale. Thinking of the waste. That crinkle on her brow getting worse and no face cream in the pot. Everyone would have gone. It would be just me and her. And I'd be too small to say anything to cheer her up.

I'd be nothing but a nuisance. Toddling about the place and picking up bits of dropped food. Stuffing it into my squishy gob. I'd be too wee to be useful for a long time, but I'd tell her I will be one day. I'd tell her stuff will get better in a few years and she won't need to wring the necks of chickens for Christmas Day. Everything will be OK one day, I'd say. I'd feed her one days like wee morsels held out to a woman who's starving.

One day, I'd say, you'll sell a thousand kitchen gadgets, and meet a man with his own business. And he'll be kind, and sort

111

of funny and daft. He'll be the sort of man who never buys jewellery for your anniversary, but surprises you with a fridge and fills it with jam. You'll love it so much you'll keep peeking inside at your preserves in a line. Shiny as rubies, the jars all lit up like stained glass. You'll be able to stop cuddling baby bunnies, loving the softness while still waiting for them to grow up into pies. You'll only keep one rabbit, I'd say. Really, that's how much better stuff will be. You'll keep him to stroke when your hands are cold and you want to touch something furry and warm. That's all.

Mostly, I'd want to tell her not to get fearty the time she caught me just outside the back door. Three years old. Wobbly on my feet. I was staring at a scrawny sparrow fallen from a branch, stroking its crooked wing, its spindly legs, all wonky and wrong. I was lifting it off the floor and holding it to my skinny chest, wanting to beat my heartbeat into it, but I couldn't. I could do nothing but hold it in my fingers. Lift it and rub its stone-cool beak against my spitty mouth. Ma caught me like this. With the bird suddenly lifting its wings and flap, flapping out of my hands. She snatched me indoors, wiped my mouth with a tissue and smacked my hands. Hard. 'Dirty! That's dirty! Don't do that ever again. That thing's full of fleas,' she said. But even though I could still feel the slap stinging, I didn't cry. I was staring at the plain brown bird, perching on the fence.

That's the moment I'd go back for if I could. I'd try to do something to let Ma know she doesn't have to worry about me so much. That, as wee I was, even if I couldn't say it right, I loved seeing that bird fly. I didn't love the dizziness, my fuzzy-feeling mouth, or her spitty tissue scrubbing off the germs. I loved this feeling I didn't have words for. I wanted to clap my chubby hands and giggle. It was like a baby realising she doesn't have to crawl. She can stand up, wobble, and walk.

Ma's clacking about the kitchen in her slippers with the fluffy pom-poms on the front. The cupboards swing open and groan. She's dragging out the Tupperware for scones to sell at the fair. God, the fair, so many mouths everywhere. I scrunch up my assignment and start all over again.

If I could go back in time, I'd visit England and have a cuppa with Henry the Eighth's wives . . . Listen, lass, I'd tell each of them, I don't think you're going to like being Queen. It's not all it's cracked up to be. There are plenty more fish to fry, and fellas for that matter. Not all of them have beards or funny hats. Quite a few of them do, mind . . .

LORRIE

The crowd gasped at the money on the counter. Joe Clark stood behind his mother scratching his plaster cast and shuffling his feet.

'No, Ma. Come on, let's go. She's just kidding.'

His fingers on her arm were flies on ham. She folded her arms. Joe fidgeted. Tall, broad, and about as handsome as a girl can stand. I had no idea why he'd want to kiss Sylvie, of all people. I'd do it for free.

Bunny and Sylvie stood with their hands on their mouths. Men whistled through their teeth. Women whispered. It was the most anyone had ever offered for a kiss that anyone could recall. The closest to it was Fraser and Bonnie Campbell, who everyone was sure would die an old maid. Quiet, and cleverer than was good for her, her head was always buried too deep into a book to look for a man. That is, until the kissing booth. Fraser had strode up and laid a note on the counter, barely able to look her in the eye. Bonnie was a librarian. He didn't own a library card. He was a fisherman. Her hands were as smooth as his were raw from rope. They were both lonely and keeping so busy most wouldn't recognise it. It was a story people still told to this day. The couple were married a year later, though they'd never spoke until that day at the fair. The story was a reminder of the advantages of the booth. Though no one admitted it, for single men and women it provided an opportunity to try someone out without suffering a dull date, or your parents starting to plan your wedding after a few matinees.

The crowd assessed Sylvie, fiddling with a doily not dissimilar to the collar of her dress, shoulders hunched, unfashionably tall. They looked at her, then at Joe. 'Oh, why not?' 'There's no harm.' 'The girl can do a lot worse.'

Bunny believed in sprinkling sugar over any pill you wanted someone to swallow. Whether it was a signature on a payment plan for kitchenware, or saying no. She walked around the cake stall to address Joe's mother with a smile and her sweetest saleswoman voice.

'Ha ha ha.' Bunny laughed. 'That's a very generous donation you have, Mrs Clark, but my daughter can't kiss anyone, I'm afraid. She's only sixteen.'

'So what? Joe's sixteen. I know plenty of folks here did a whole lot more at that age.'

The crowd shifted. Men inspected the knots on their shoelaces, hoping their teenage sweethearts wouldn't be dug up in the presence of the wife. Women herded their kids away for ice cream and bags of honeycomb. On the island, no one forgot anything about anyone, they simply stopped talking about certain things.

Mrs Clark was the sort of customer Bunny had encountered before, a woman who wasn't afraid to thrust an airtight plastic pot back in her face, grab a rusty tin from the kitchen and say, 'I was raised storing stuff in old biscuit tins, I'll die with biscuit tins. I don't need your swanky crap.'

Bunny would always offer such customers another product to peruse, an egg whisk, or perhaps something to core an apple. She searched the faces of the crowd.

'Perhaps another girl would be happy to oblige, someone less shy . . .'

I clutched the lip balm in my pocket, ready to say, 'Well, it *is* for charity, I suppose.' If I could kiss anyone it would be Zach, but, since he barely looked in my direction, Joe Clark would do. I was ready to kiss someone, and he was pretty. I could step up and be his consolation prize. It could change our lives. Joe would step back with the look of a man who went out to buy a bicycle and drove off in a Rolls-Royce. It was the sort of story couples dine out on for years. A decade from now, Joe could say, 'To think, if I'd got the girl I thought I wanted, we wouldn't be so happy today.'

'One kiss. Sylvie Johnson, or I take my money home.' Mrs Clark folded her arms and her chest doubled in size. She straightened up and stood still, a monument to the lengths a woman will go to for her son.

AN EVALUATION OF AILEEN CLARK

Nose: The beetroots she pulls out on her land leave her hands blushing, her fingers have the aroma of coins she drops into a pickle jar after selling the vegetables and eggs to the grocer. On a good day, you can smell only soap on her, but on a day with a breeze there's no escaping the chicken shit ground into the soles of her shoes after she cleans out the coop, yet again.

Palate: If a voice could tell people what someone's been eating, the woman ate only chicory, radishes and sour cream. This is a woman who was promised the moon and wound up with windows so grubby she couldn't see out. It is difficult to believe there was ever a man in her life. 'The fairies got him one night' is as much as anyone says about him. No one in the village speaks his name in her presence. They wouldn't dare. It wasn't wise to make the woman angry. Once, years ago, Seth Johnson's son overcharged her for paint. Whenever the hardware store comes up in conversation, she still brings this up, certain the owner is a crook, instructing the boy to dish out the wrong change all the time, to make a few more pennies each day.

Finish: The woman is ready to wrestle. Her hands are leather, her tongue is a whip. More than would care to speak of it recall being on its sharp end. Mostly mothers whose kids had called Mrs Clark's son hopalong at nursery. The children were young. They knew no better, their mothers claimed. Everyone knows better than they let on, Mrs Clark would reply, teach your kids some manners or I'll teach you some.

Overall: A woman who makes holding a grudge an art form. She stands beside her son oblivious to his shame, willing to fight for him until the last tooth in her head. It was strange to see her speak about kissing. The woman's demeanour made people think she'd pucker up to nothing, never had, or would in her life.

'It's that girl or nothing.' Aileen Clark pointed at Sylvie. 'Don't ask me why her. I've seen bigger lips on a trout,' she said, 'but it's her he's stuck on. I'm sick of him mooching around, scribbling stupid little poems for her, all of it. Let him kiss her and get it out of his system.'

We saw that, to Mrs Clark, kisses were as simple as the chocolates in the confectioner's window, irresistible when you peered in carrying a sack of potatoes from the grocers. You could save up to buy one, take one bite and walk on. They were never as luscious as they looked in the display. The craving was cured by having a nibble, then you were done.

'Ma, it's OK. I don't want Sylvie if she doesn't want me. I hate this, let's go.'

Joe's cheeks were as pink as someone in a play. His mother failed to notice. Men muttered 'what's the harm . . .' Women shook their heads: 'if the lass doesn't want to . . .' Joe reminded them of a hundred good-looking boys who wouldn't look at them twice. They saw his rejection as a victory for plain girls everywhere. Handsome or not, Sylvie was the one girl Joe couldn't get. And she was one of their own.

Mrs Clark faced Sylvie, wild-eyed with rage. 'So you won't give him a peck? Not even for charity? You better than him? What's wrong with him?'

'It's not that there's anything wrong with him, Mrs Clark,' Bunny interrupted. 'I'm sure he's a lovely lad. It's just – '

'Look at my boy right now and tell me what's wrong with him.'

'Ma, stop it. I'm not kidding.' Joe pulled an arm. 'It's time to go.'

The crowd parted, pretending not to overhear Mrs Clark's voice jabbing through.

'Snooty cow . . . That Bunny Johnson is a self-righteous fu . . . '

The crowd slowly dispersed. People made their way to the swingboats, the ice-cream van, and the tombola. Bunny clapped her hands, returning to the business side of her stall.

'Right, the show's over. Come on,' she called, 'who's got a sweet tooth? We still have plenty of cake for sale! I know someone took a slice and didn't pay.'

I'm just there with Ma faffing about with the sponges, arranging the shiny cherries on the top. Licking my sticky fingers. Looking anywhere but in the direction of kisses. There's this wizened-looking fella on the other side of the field. The one I saw that morning outside Lorrie's. He's so skinny his shirt's hanging off his collarbones without touching his chest. He looks like he's scowling, though I can't see his mouth. His moustache is so bushy his lips must have retired from yattering.

He climbs the fence when he sees Lorrie's family arrive. He's clutching the bag of sausages he's bought to his chest and making a break for it. It doesn't look easy. The gnarly fence snags his shirt. He pulls himself over it with stickman arms that might snap. I'm wondering why he'd go to all that bother instead of just using the gate. Then the whole island starts gawping at me.

It's worse than when they dragged out Resusci Annie at Brownies. The lassies all huddled around itching for a First Aid badge. Pinch her nose. Clear an airway. Breathe. They all took their turn saving a plasticky life. Then it was up to me. I put my fingers into the rubber mouth to check for sweets or false teeth and I couldn't breathe. The disinfectant reeked and everyone was gawping. My stomach was churning. I kept thinking about Ma smacking my knees. I didn't save Annie that day, instead I puked all over her. I never went to Brownies again. The kids made pukey sounds when they saw me all year.

God, the whole world's looking at me, and all I can think about is Brownies. I'm sweating lochs and my palms are redder and claggier than the cherries on the cakes. Don't look up, don't even move. I freeze like if I'm still enough folks will look through me and just see Victoria sponge. I was always doing that when I was wee. Ma would tell me to get out of her sight and I'd cover my eyes with my fingers. Frozen. Invisible unless I moved an inch, in my wee head anyway.

I stare over the stall at the grass. Mrs Clark has the smallest brown feather snagged to a silver buckle on her shoe. It wavers in the wind. Back and forth. Back and forth. There's a toy soldier lying by her foot too. It probably fell out of the pocket of some laddie off and away to hook a duck. I focus on it until Mrs Clark turns and her foot presses the private into the dirt. I bow my head and sneak a peek through my fringe at Joe walking away.

He's looking at me and mouthing a slow *sorry*. And it seems no one's whispering with candyfloss tongues. It's just me and him reading each other's lips through the crowd. I know Joe's sorry. And he knows I'm grateful he convinced his mother to leave. He trails behind her like the sickly wee laddie he used to be is still inside him. He'll never outrun that kid no matter what he does. He'll always be there somewhere, and he'll never make his Ma see him any other way. I reckon I know how he feels.

God, I'd kiss him right now if I could, just for placing his bandaged hand on his mother's shoulder and steering her away. I'd lean over the cheese scones and place my lips on his until he closed his eyes and the world fell away. If kissing was anything like the movies anyway. But, it's not and I can't. All I can do is wipe my claggy hands on my skirt and push slices of pie into smaller circles on the crumby plates.

LORRIE

The year was split for Domestic Science. Girls orbited around cooking and sewing while the boys made pine bird boxes and steel shoehorns that snagged their mother's stockings. Sylvie wasn't in my group. It was a relief not to be saddled with her. Our classmates were all whispering after the fair. Sylvie Johnson wasn't all that. That girl thought she kept the sun in her underwear. Who does she think she is? Poor Joe, with his broken fingers, left standing, in front of everyone. He was so talented too. Everyone remembered him being the only redeeming feature of last year's school show, with his guitar and a voice sweeter than a hot toddy on an icy day.

Joe was so admired it seemed Sylvie had posted a memo on the blackboard to us all:

A NOTE TO EVERY GIRL IN CLASS
Your dreams aren't good enough for me. I'm better than you.

Blair Munro couldn't sew a straight seam or keep a straight face. We shared a workbench for sewing. The class project was to make a nightdress. Girls sat in rows pinning lacy collars onto gifts for their mothers. Blair sucked her cotton, did a few tacks in gauzy cerise fabric and placed her foot on the pedal of the Singer, revving it, wishing it was a motorbike.

'You'll have to be careful with the tension if you want to work with that sort of fabric,' Miss Stone said. 'Besides, you're not ready for machine work yet, Blair. It all needs to be tacked *properly*.' Miss Stone nudged the curls on her shoulder, a woman full of gestures that resembled poses for photographs no one was around to take. If she hadn't wound up being a teacher, she could have been a movie star. She had the sort of face that was ready for a close-up, and she wore homemade clothes that resembled woollier, more winter-proof versions of creations in *Vogue*. Looking at her, I thought: I'm going to be a woman like that when I grow up, but without the dot of red ink on my cuff.

The class all brought in similar fabric for their nightgowns; pastels, or plain white cotton, accompanied by embroidery thread and sketches of rosebuds to sew onto the collar. That is, everyone except Blair and Marjorie Swift. Marjorie's father was an upholsterer. He didn't see why his daughter should fork out for fabric when he had plenty spare in his workshop. Marjorie winced pushing pins into a fabric strong enough to cover a chair. It was the sturdiest nightdress anyone ever saw. Wearing it, Marjorie's mother would be part woman, part sofa. Marjorie knew this, but gritted her teeth and grabbed a second thimble. Blair laughed at her, flapping her own nightdress in the air.

'You can see right through it,' I said. 'You'll catch your death.'

'Someone's bound to keep you warm wearing this.' Blair winked.

She wasn't what I'd call a vamp, not when she was stationary. The freckles on her nose were orange. Her skin was silvery and breakable-looking as a doll. But when she moved she was shatterproof. She flicked her hair, crossed her legs and swung her feet under the bench, restless, ready to charge out as soon as the bell rang.

AN EVALUATION OF BLAIR MUNRO

Nose: The bubblegum she snaps between her front teeth compliments her face. She does it so often. Whenever she isn't impressed. The scent covers the faint waft of the cigarettes she sneaks out for between classes. When she returns, she spritzes perfume on her neck in the corridor to cover the smell, pleating more gum into her mouth. Juicy Fruit.

Palate: The chips she slips out to share with mechanics at lunchtime, the dandelion and burdock that fizzes up the paper straw she's willing to share without wiping off the spit. There's a certain laugh that bubbles out of her in the presence of boys. It is only for the company of the opposite sex and it can stop as fast as it starts. She snaps her gum again, making a point of trying to be unimpressed by their jokes. She turns away mid-punchline, suddenly bored. She doesn't need to hear more. She can laugh just fine on her own.

Finish: Coppery as a kettle, freckle-coloured hair, a red purse and skirts she borrows off her mother as frequently as her lighter. Whatever day it is, Blair appears to be popping into school on her way to somewhere kids aren't allowed. Everyone wants to follow her there, take her hand and be lead.

Overall: That girl you want to be, but don't know how to become. Failing that, just knowing her will do. Blair's friendship was a red dress I wasn't sure I should wear. I tried it on without being sure if I could get away with it.

I lit a cigarette behind the school kitchens after class, air rippling out of the vents in the wall warming our legs. Blair didn't believe in matches. Finding someone to give her a light provided too many opportunities to strike up a conservation with whoever she chose. I flicked a flame from the lighter I stole from my father's jacket and cupped it with my palm.

'I didn't know you smoked.'

I shrugged. I'd tried my first cigarette a week ago. I wasn't keen on the dizziness, the flavour, or the aroma, but I loved the lighter. It was gold-coloured, shiny and smooth. I loved the excuse it gave me to bump into Blair.

'Have you got a boyfriend?' Blair blew a slow smoke ring. We watched it linger and fray.

'Do you?'

'Sometimes, when I feel like it . . .'

'Who needs one full-time?'

Blair grinned. I'd passed some sort of test. Our schoolmates were starting to filter out of the building for lunch. They sat with paper bags on the grass and clustered in groups. I spotted Sylvie clutching her lunchbox by the gate, standing so awkwardly she reminded me of a child having her height measured against a door.

'Is that your pal?' Blair asked. 'That Sylvie? Isn't she the one who bit a chicken at a funeral or something?'

'No.'

'That's what I heard.'

'She's not really my friend.' I flicked ash. 'She just lives next door.'

Sylvie started to eat lunch alone. I observed her at a distance, spreading out her coat, polishing her apple, peeling the crusts off her bread. It occurred to me I didn't have to sit with her. I didn't have to do anything. I knew Blair Munro.

I could feel the difference almost instantly, a stirring of curiosity directed my way. I'd become interesting, for doing nothing but knowing someone everyone wanted to know.

'Are you still friends with Sylvie?' Marjorie Swift asked in the changing rooms after hockey. 'I keep seeing you skulking off for a smoke with Blair. Have you been to Blair's house? What's it like? I heard her mother plays Patsy Cline all day and has parties all night.'

I smiled, as if I knew more than I did, letting on that I was closer to Blair than I was. I spent the remainder of the day making a point of looking out the window, pretending to consider nothing but the bell, and the hundred plans after school everyone wished I'd include them in.

I'm waiting for Lorrie to notice I'm dead different. I keep faffing around with my fringe. She won't look. We're popping to
the café where they squirt a smidge more raspberry into the
milkshakes just for us. I'm putting a couple of songs on the
jukebox and staring out at the black-headed gulls. They're all
willing to give up a wee bit of their wildness for a few chips
tossed their way. I slide my feet under the table and wonder
how to dance to 'Purple People Eater'. I won't dance until we're
alone though. Just me and Lorrie, in our bedrooms on a dreich
day. It's the only way I can do it. When anyone's looking I move
like a robot, but in my head I glide like a swan.

I don't wanna admit I waited for Lorrie at lunch again. I
stood staring at the pavement dotted with ants doing a conga
around a dropped chocolate lime. I watched them for ages.
It was better than looking across the field and seeing Lorrie
yattering with Blair. She can have more pals than one. Not
everyone has to like me. I know, but when I see Lorrie with
someone who hates me my stomach gets this feeling like a
wrung-out dishcloth.

Blair's one of those lassies who makes a face whenever she
passes me. 'Nice dress, Sylvie,' she says. And she thinks I'm
too daft to realise that when some people say 'nice' it means
stinking.

'I missed you at lunchtime.'

Shite. I didn't want to say anything. I bite my lip and feel teeth digging in.

'Oh, I was working on that stupid nightie,' Lorrie says.

'Oh. With Blair? She's beautiful.'

'I suppose.'

'Do you like my hair?' I ask. I hate myself as soon as I say it. Hate sniffing around for a compliment. Lorrie looks at me, finally. I've let my hair down like she always says I should. I've smoothed it behind one ear, instead of scraping my ponytail back so tight Lorrie says just looking gives her a migraine.

'You look fine,' she says.

Then she carries on chattering. Blair this . . . Blair that . . . Blair says . . . Blair helps her mother at work after school. One time, she found a necklace. A gold one, a heart. Another time, a bracelet. She let Blair keep them both.

We leave the café and dawdle past the shops painted in Easter colours. It's only by the harbour where all the paintwork isn't white. Pink. Lavender. Lemon. Mint. The shops facing the sea are defiant with colour, damned if all that weather whipping their faces is going to stop them looking cheery. The shop owners gripe about painting the walls every year. They swear they'll just let it peel, then paint it again anyway. Whenever we're here, me and Lorrie point at our favourite paint jobs and wonder what colours we'd paint our own houses one day. Baby blue for Lorrie. Yellow for me. Today Lorrie doesn't mention the paint. Blair's made her snow-blind. The lure of the lass is too bright to see anything.

I push my hair behind my ear ten thousand times and still forget to put it in a ponytail before I get in. Ma spots it as soon as she sets eyes on me and follows me to my room with the linen.

'What's with this?' She strokes a strand of my hair. 'This isn't for that lad's benefit is it?'

'No, Ma. I just wanted to be different.'

It's the first time we've really been alone since the day of the fair. Without being aware of Seth and Zach downstairs anyway. Ma can finally let rip.

'What got into that woman? Mrs Clark. Is there something going on with Joe I should know about?'

Ma looks at me relentlessly. The fresh bedding is piled high in her arms. There's a loose strand of cotton on a hem. If I pulled it a whole line of stitching would undo.

'Nothing's going on.'

'You must have done something to lead the boy on. These things don't come from nowhere.'

'I haven't done anything. I can't control what folk think of me,' I say.

Ma bundles the sheets off my bed and flaps on the fresh one. I fold a hospital corner opposite her, crisp as a sealed envelope.

'Don't lie to me, Sylvie. There'll be consequences. I don't want you seeing that boy. Promise me you haven't.'

I shake a pillow so hard a couple of feathers fly and land on the pillowcase.

'I promise. I have nothing to do with Joe Clark, Ma. I'd never lie to you, cross my heart.'

Ma nods. 'Make sure it stays that way.' She places the last cover on the bed and says, 'I really do love this washing powder, don't you? It smells so much fresher than the other one, like a meadow.' She leaves to make the other beds become meadows. I breathe. It's over for now.

LORRIE

Rook Cutler knocked off from the distillery and popped his head around the door. The day had been endless. It started with a pigeon on the step, stone cold. Grumps covered the silvery rainbow on its throat with a cloth and muttered. 'Looks like the bastard's running out of owls.' My mother wasn't letting it go, not this time. Even at dinner it was still on her mind. It was only a baby, poor thing. It still didn't have all its proper flight feathers. She demanded to know who would do this. It must stop. She'd seen more dead birds than a woman could stand.

'Birds die,' Grumps said, dipping a cracker into a jar of beetroot.

'Not in the same place all the time. There was one last month too. Why here? You know who's leaving them here, don't you? Why don't you call the police?'

'And tell them what? Birds die? I think they already know that, Cora. Don't worry about it. He's harmless. Crazy, but harmless.'

'Who?'

Grumps started to whistle. The conversation was officially over. He could live with dead birds more than the breaking of rules he'd lived his whole life by:

1. Do what you have to do to get by
2. Respect your family
3. Choose your friends wisely

4. Tell nobody nothing, not even the police. No one respects a telltale
5. It's Us against Them

It wasn't always clear who exactly *Them* really was, but in any given circumstance there was always a Them.

Rook grinned watching Grumps and my mother talk, enjoying their voices, the ordinary reassurance of how they were always the same.

'I'm away for the day,' he said. 'See you in the morning.'

'Stay for supper, what's the rush?' Grumps said.

There was nothing stopping Rook staying a while. There was no wife waiting for him in his cottage on the south side of the island. No children wanted him to fix their bikes. Nothing waited for him but the wild deer he hunted, and the pots he put out for langoustine. He took a step into the kitchen and took a step out when my father stepped into the room.

'No, really I'd better be going.'

'You better had,' my father said.

'I'll be seeing you on Monday, Lucky.'

My mother smiled, though she knew as soon as Rook left her husband would say, 'What does he still call you Lucky for anyway? It's ridiculous. You're not a kid any more.'

I grabbed my bag, seizing my chance to make my escape in the shuffle of someone else leaving. 'I'd better be going too.'

It was Friday. I'd wolfed down oatcakes, lacking the patience to sit through dinner. The endless waiting. Toby's pointless facts about milk and cabbage, my mother's boundless interest in his random facts. I was starting to see her fascination in whatever he had to say wasn't what it seemed. She wasn't that interested in the life of Houdini. She was more interested in filling the silence. So long as my brother was talking, it was less obvious she and her husband had little to say.

'Hold on missy, not so fast! Where did you say you're going?' she asked.

'I'm working on a sewing project with my friend, Blair. I already told you.'

'You're not much of a sewer, Lorrie. Can't her mother help her?'

'Blair's mother lost her hand,' I said. I don't know why. It would be a difficult lie to keep up. Suddenly, my heart was beating fast. If she ever met Blair's mother, I'd have to say it grew back, or insist she must be thinking of somebody else.

'Oh, that's awful!' My mother touched her collarbone. 'How did it happen?'

'Boating accident,' I said. 'A couple of years ago. Blair's never had fish since, her mother won't have it in the house.'

I was back on track. My mother was horrified picturing fingers in propellers, a life without trout. Whenever I mentioned Blair from now on, she'd scour a pan, knead scones or scrub the counter vigorously, afraid that if she didn't use her hands to their full extent something might take them away.

'And someone's dropping you off later? I don't want you walking in all weathers.'

I dragged myself closer to the door, pretending I wasn't desperate to race out of it.

'They wouldn't need to if I could take the car.'

Grumps stroked his chin, remembering our lessons around and around the distillery where the trucks dropped off the grain.

'You could take my pick-up.'

'She's not driving anywhere until she has her licence,' my mother said.

I sulked enough to make them glad to see the back of my lying behind. I was finally out of there. I'd been dreaming of this forever. Tonight, I was going on my first date and I couldn't wait.

The rattling at my door sounds kinda funny. *Clank, clank, clank.* Zach's knocking with a chain in his fist. I've got it into my head I want the canary's cage to swing from a hoop by the window. I want it to be able to peek up at the sky and pretend to fly. Zach scores a cross on the ceiling with the pencil that lives in his shirt pocket. I sit on the rocker keeping him company.

'I haven't seen your pal this week,' he says.

He knows her name fine well, but he's refusing to say it. I wonder why.

'Lorrie,' I say.

'Aye, Lorrie. I saw her all dressed up as if she was going dancing or something.' The hook screws into the ceiling. Bits of plaster sprinkle onto the birdcage like a dusting of snow.

'She's always dolled up,' I say. 'It's just how she is.'

'What do you lasses do anyway? Just listen to music? What sort of stuff does she like?'

'Urm . . . everything, anything, so long as she can dance to it. What do you care anyway?'

'I don't. I'm just making conversation.'

Zach hangs up the cage and goes. The canary hops around the swing, not sure it's safe to get on. It's not like that lad to make conversation. The only thing he normally makes is a mess in the kitchen with his sandwiches. Marmalade on brown bread. Always crumbs all over the shop. Not a plate in sight.

That's it! I reckon there's a reason he wants to chat. Lorrie. Just last week he caught me carrying glasses downstairs after she'd gone and said, 'Milkshake, again? Raspberry? It's always the same. Is it Lorrie's favourite or something?'

I never noticed before, but he likes her, I think. Or he's thinking about liking her, anyway. Gathering snippets of information like a horny squirrel and deciding if he likes what he finds. Wow! They could start courting. Then get married. And Lorrie would be like my sister and we'd be friends until we're old ladies who keep our teeth in a glass. Or, I reckon, it could go the other way. God, they could start courting, then fall out and hate each other forever. And Lorrie would never come here ever again.

I wonder if I should tell her? Naw. Bollocks to that. It would make her unbearable, that's if she still likes him, anyway. I don't know if she does. If she did, I reckon she wouldn't be going out with someone else. I'm not supposed to know, but I do. She's been whispering about it with Blair all week. I keep seeing them giggling and shushing, shush, shush shush like two lassies in a contest for impersonating the sea. 'What am I going to wear? Shall I curl my hair?' It doesn't take a genius to figure it out. Lorrie can't keep a secret like me. I know her way better than she thinks.

LORRIE

I struggled to blink coming out of Blair's room. I was wearing so much mascara my lashes were zipped together. I was surprised Blair hadn't put on a coat and snuck out without anyone seeing she was wearing a bullet bra. It never occurred to her. She strolled into the lounge carrying her jacket over her arm.

'Don't you girls look cracking.' Mrs Munro glanced up from a mirror magnifying her pores, tweezers perched over her eyebrows.

The cottage was nothing like anyone could imagine from the outside. The outside was the same as any other: slate-roofed, stony and crouched. The inside was fluffy with shagpile, the coffee table was kidney-shaped. The wooden beams were covered with postcards of movies, and most of the furniture was lined against the walls, making room to dance. Unlike every room I'd ever been in, the chairs didn't all face the fire. They tilted towards the glow of the jukebox filling one wall. Mrs Munro put down her tweezers and got up to select a song.

'Do you like it, isn't she a beauty?' She ran a finger along the glass display, one eyebrow plucked into surprise, one down to earth. 'I got it from a fella who knocked me off my bicycle. The one who owns that pub on the other side of the island. "What will it take not to get the police involved?" he asked, "What've you got?" I said. He was seven sheets to the wind. I've still got still a funny bump where I went over. Look.' She held out her hand to show me the egg of one wrist bone so much bigger than the other. 'But hey, it's worth it. I couldn't live without my music.'

She laughed the sort of laugh that drags along anybody who hears it. Blair took a cigarette from her handbag. Mrs Munro didn't blink. The pair reminded me of roommates more than mother and daughter. I'd never known anybody with parents like hers, parents who put being friends before anything else. I still don't.

'You going somewhere nice tonight?' Blair asked.

'I'm going out for a mussel supper with someone who owns a carpet-cleaning business,' Mrs Munro replied. 'I was hoping he could sort out that rug.'

We took a moment of silence to consider the rug where red wine went to die. Looking at it, I noticed the shag pile carpet beneath it didn't fit wall to wall. It was patched together with offcuts from the hotel where Mrs Munro worked. The mints in the Murano glass bowl came from the same place, so did the books of matches she left lying around.

'So, how about you?' Mrs Munro asked. 'What are your plans?'

'We're meeting a couple of guys I know,' said Blair.

There was no need for her to lie. Mrs Munro made no demands. My parents would have insisted on being introduced to whoever wanted the pleasure of my company. Any potential date would be forced to suffer Toby's pointless facts about liver, my mother's cooking, and my father's silence, before they had permission to take me anywhere. It didn't seem a fair trade.

The island had a shortage of places we could go to with our dates. The only cinema was Movie Night in the village. Fraser Campbell sometimes set up a projector in the church and his wife would make popcorn and wander down the aisle selling it in paper bags. It was rare their friend in England could get his hands on a 'damaged' film anyone had ever heard of. But occasionally the projectionist sent gold: *Frankenstein*, *The Wolf Man*, even *The Wizard of Oz*. People cheered so loudly when Dorothy got home, Fraser smiled, let the credits roll and put on the film again from the start. Wherever I went, for months, I'd hear someone thinking about it. Farmers whistled 'If I Only Had a Heart', rounding up their sheep. Children plodded to school whispering about lions, tigers, and bears. Even our teacher, Miss Stone, hummed 'Somewhere Over the Rainbow' while she wandered around making sure no one was cheating on their exams. Everyone in the village crammed into the church for a movie. It was no place for couples to hold hands.

There were no dance halls to attend either. The island offered would-be lovers no entertainment but a bar in the hotel on the south side, and the café that stayed open late on Fridays.

Blair and I waited outside it, the wind lifting our hair and making our faces sting. The sign over the café was blank and had been for over a month. Elizabeth Roe had been cleaning the windows one day when she'd noticed something she hadn't before. She rushed in to tell her husband with the wet rag still in her hand, dripping all over the floor.

'This place doesn't have a name!' she said.

'Eh? What are you on about, woman?' Harvey replied. 'Of course it does.'

'It doesn't, not really, come see.' She dragged Harvey outside, a few customers following with their hands in their pockets, curious to see what all the fuss was about. They looked up at the sign over the door: CAFÉ. That's all it said, nothing more. There was only one café on the island, so there'd never been a reason to give it a name. Elizabeth had never thought about it before, but it bothered her now. The place was their baby, lavished with all the love and attention they had planned on giving to the children they hadn't been blessed with. It should have had a christening. How had she never noticed before?

She scraped the ladder across the path. Customers sipping their tea looked up at her wellies as she got out a paintbrush and whitewashed over the sign.

'There,' Elizabeth said, 'it's all ready for a proper name to be painted on now.'

Just what that name would be had been open to debate. Harvey had suggested *Harvey's Place* and was met with a glare. He changed tack, suggesting *Beautiful Elizabeth's Café* instead, and fared no better. 'You have no imagination. Leave it to me,' she said, making a cup of coffee so strong her husband couldn't drink it without gurning.

It was a recent development, later closing on Fridays. Elizabeth Roe had a soft spot for musicians and let one play most weekends, as long as they promised to include a Johnny Cash song. 'More trouble than it's worth,' she would say every week, sweeping dropped crisps and spilled cola off the floor. 'Who'd have thought people who came to hear ballads of love and murder could make such a mess? This is the last straw, it isn't worth it.' She would swear off music night until the next guy came in with a scruffy guitar case and a bellyful of hope. Joe Clark played once, before he bust his hand. By all accounts he was good, though I didn't see him myself. Bunny wouldn't let Sylvie out after six. I stayed in and kept her company that night, rather than let her feel she was missing out. That, and I'd had a cold sore that was visible through my lipstick.

The boys rocked up twenty minutes after Blair and I arrived. The first thing I noticed was they weren't wearing ties. The second thing I noticed was they weren't strictly boys. They were older than us and they were mechanics. Looking at them, I could have guessed. Their jeans had deep pockets, their fingernails were only just clean. Their quiffs were oily and dark.

'Evening, ladies.' The gangly one grinned, a slither of it was for me, the lion's share was Blair's. The shorter one and I looked at one another in wordless realisation: oh, this one must be mine. Blair pointed at the shorter guy, then at me, tying us together with a swirl of her finger. 'This is Lorrie. Lorrie, this is Cal.' Her date was called Dobby. I supposed it was his surname. He looked like a Dobby. Looking at him, it was possible to imagine headmasters barking that name, sergeants drilling it into him, bosses yelling it across the garage, and no one ever whispering it.

Blair and I were careful not to snag our stockings on the wrought-iron table. We sat in the corner of the café. Boys on one side of the table, girls on the other. Blair knew Dobby well. They joked and poked fun at one another in the manner of a couple who know they don't have to behave to be liked. We ordered fizzy drinks while Cal and I made the sort of small talk that lets you get to know someone, but not well. What sort of music do you listen to? What do you do? What do you do for fun? How long have you two been friends? Cal had known Dobby all his life. When they weren't changing brake pads, they would take their boats out around the island.

AN EVALUATION OF CAL JAMESON

Notes: The arcs of his fingernails are shiny and black – motor oil mingled with the Brylcreem in his hair. He runs his hand through it often, strutting up his quiff, slick as a peacock with its feathers raised. It's hard to imagine his laugh doesn't coat his mouth with treacle, it's so sticky and dark there's no way to describe it as anything but dirty. It spills out with a joke I don't understand. I smile anyway – a woman of the world.

Palate: He tastes of the snifter of drink he keeps in a crocodile-covered hip flask, cola, and the lip gloss of a dozen girls his friend has set him up with before. There's a wry twist to his mouth, bitter at recalling polite dinners served by the parents of girls. They always asked what his father does for a living and his reply would taste sour in his mouth: 'I don't know. If I ever meet him, I'll ask him.' He is tired of thanking strangers for a lovely meal, knowing he'll never be invited again. Boys like him don't deserve nice girls. To date him, a girl must slip off her heels and sneak out after dark.

Finish: He slips his overalls off at 5 p.m. in favour of jeans and shirts he refuses to fasten to the neck – a buttoned-up collar is one step off a desk job, a leash cutting in. Not in this lifetime, not him. Until his apprenticeship is served odd jobs supplement his wage. There's always someone around who wants something doing but doesn't want to get their hands dirty. He's the man for the job.

Overall: That variety of boy it isn't possible to imagine having said please, not once in his life.

Cal wanted to know if I'd ever been out to any of the other islands dotted around the coast. Some were inhabited by nothing but pods of seals and, some said, selkies. Others had small populations who did things their own way.

'There's a whole other world out there,' Cal said.

'I've never been,' I said. 'Grumps, my grandfather, put me off. The people who live there aren't friendly, he says. Outsiders aren't welcome.'

'True, locals can be a bit cagey, but, I don't know . . .' Cal fidgeted with the menu and considered the fried squid. 'You have to respect anyone who lives there in all seasons. They follow their own rules. It's beautiful. I'll show you one day.' He drummed his fingers on the table, impatient with the service, or at how slow getting to know someone is – I couldn't tell. 'So, what do you want to be when you grow up?' he asked.

'Happy,' I said. It wasn't true. I wanted to be a femme fatale – stylish, rich, famous. I wanted to be special somehow. But once, when I'd asked Sylvie what she wanted to be she'd replied 'happy'. That was all. I'd liked the sound of it.

'That's the coolest answer to that boring question I've ever fucking heard,' Cal said.

Elizabeth Roe came over with a notepad. 'Everything OK, kids?' she asked. 'Anything else I can get you?'

'A portion of chips,' Cal said.

'Go on, ask him, ask them all,' Harvey Roe was calling across the café to his wife.

Elizabeth rolled her eyes. 'Give me a minute, the poor kids are starving. They just want chips! They don't want to be bothered by us. They're on a date – look at them, it's written all over them.'

'Just ask.' Harvey put down his spatula and came over to us. 'Hey, kids, which is better do you think, as a name for the café: the Ugly Mermaid or the Hungry Squid?'

Elizabeth sighed. 'Ignore my husband, he's been asking everyone who walks in the door!'

'I like the mermaid,' said Cal.

'Not sure about the ugly,' Dobby said. 'What about the Busty Mermaid?' His hands made the shape of a pin-up. Blair whacked his arm.

'Ha! Another vote for the mermaid anyway!' Elizabeth said.

Harvey marked another line on the chalkboard where he usually wrote the specials. Today, a squid and a mermaid were using the space to fight to the death.

I ate off the same plate as Cal and wondered if I could ever fall in love with him. Probably, at the same time I wasn't sure he was someone I'd ever really like. He linked his arm into mine as we left, our fingers slick with the chips we'd dipped into a puddle of ketchup.

'What about the Happy Squid?' Harvey called after us, his wife swatting him with a rolled-up newspaper.

'Ignore him, kids, he just hates to lose!'

We agreed to meet again the following Friday. Dobby showed us to a car only an optimist wouldn't call a wreck and wedged a screwdriver in the door.

'Only way she'll open,' he said. 'She needs a bit of loving, but she flies.'

'She won't fly like mine,' Cal replied.

'Oh yeah? Wanna bet?'

We disappeared then, Blair and me. It was a moment for our dates and their contest of who could fix up the best wreck. Blair climbed into the car, the wind whipping a sheet of her hair covered in hairspray across her face. I ran, the scarf around my neck lifting and streaming off across the street. I chased the rippling chiffon in my kitten heels.

'Lorrie?' Zach clutched a crate of bottles under one arm. 'What are you doing here?'

'Oh, I lost my scarf.'

I didn't need to ask what brought him here. On Fridays, Zach did the beer run for the card game while the older men bickered about the stakes and who got the wobbly chair. I clutched my scarf. Zach glanced at Cal and Blair rolling down the window.

'Come on, Lorrie!' she yelled. 'What you waiting for?'

I ran to the car, praying Zach wouldn't tell Sylvie he'd ever seen me. Sylvie might tell her mother, who might tell my parents I hadn't been sewing at Blair's house after all. The rusty car started with a jerk, a puff of smoke coughing out of the exhaust. I looked out at Zach. Everything looked just as it was to him, I was sure. I was on a date with someone else. Being caught made me feel I was cheating, if not on Zach, then myself.

13TH MAY 1960

WHAT WILL YOU BE IN TEN YEARS' TIME?

In ten years from now I'll be a nun. I'll live in a convent and get into sing-songs with women who grow their own scran. There'll be apples to peel, pears, and plums. The fruit will grow behind a huge wall surrounding the convent. The walls will shade us from seeing ambulances and folks toppling over in the street. The sisters will be nifty with a knife. They'll chop fruit like holy samurai warriors and never cut themselves. We'll all be rosy with digging. And cautious when we wash the glasses and cups. There'll be no mirrors in the convent to crack. If our faces aren't pretty, we won't have a clue. Our kisses will only be for the apples we pick and polish on our chests with our breath. The order will know about singing, and jam making, and prayer, and hard work. We'll all be pals and laugh at just about anything as long as it's holy. We'll laugh a lot. Our lives will be small. And there'll be loads of stuff we don't know, but that's OK. We'll all be dead good at learning to shrug and say, 'the world is a mysterious place'.

When I'm a nun Ma will still go to the hairdressers every six weeks. She'll sit there listening to women under the driers slipping wee photos of their daughters and grandbabbies out of their purses. They'll all be comparing who's the bonniest and who married the best man.

'My daughter's a nun,' Ma will say, and Bam! All conversation will stop. The women will all shut up for bit to think about it. It's

a wonderful thing. Cracking, aye. It's also sad. What can anyone really say about that? There'll be nothing for it but to change the subject to kitchen gadgets. The Wonder Spinner for salads, the latest Tupperware pot, big enough to store a human head. Ma would love that, I reckon.

I scribble a wee sketch of a nun and surround it in inky flames. That's me, who I'll become. I'm practising now, sitting on my tod in my cell while other folk are swanning about.

It's dark now, or something close to it. It won't be long until it stops truly getting dark at night. In June, it will only get duskier. The sky is a shelf of dark blues and silhouettes starting to lose their sharp edges when Lorrie gets out of the car with her date. They face each other, making small talk. Wondering if the bird they can hear is about to shite on their heads, or declaring their undying love for each other, I can't tell. The lad bows his head and kisses her for long enough to persuade her to put her bag down on the car roof. Then Lorrie pulls away, latches the gate and flits off, wiping her mouth.

I wonder what it's like to have to put down whatever you're carrying for a kiss. It looks nowt like the kisses Lorrie used to practise on her hand like she was giving the kiss of life to a sock puppet. It looks like something charging through you, making you realise you can't be doing with carrying your pens and wet-weather hats any more. I picture Joe Clark's sulky mouth and licking it into a wee smile. I shiver. It's alright. When I'm a nun I won't think this way.

I shove my assignment in the drawer. In a decade, I'll be Sister Sylvie and Lorrie will be loved. Being loved is something she's auditioning for now, I suppose. I reckon that's all courting is, just a series of small auditions. On second thoughts, I place my *What I'll Be in 10 Years* on the desk, so Ma can spot it and never have the foggiest about the funny thoughts that spin around my head.

LORRIE

I've never been sure precisely when my father went missing. No one is. He got up, brushed his teeth, put on his ferry uniform, polished the buttons, the same as always, and left. I don't know if he'd already decided this was the night he wouldn't return, or if something decided it for him on the way.

It had been a crazy week at the distillery; a batch of rare single malt was finally ready. Grumps held a labelling party similar to the ones his father had hosted. Men and women came from all over the island to slap labels on bottles in exchange for a few bottles to stash away for Christmas. The distillery was awash with chatter and laughter, small samples of the whisky being passed around. It was so loud we could hear it along the lane. My mother had been at the distillery all week, consulting order lists, screwing on lids, and dragging away the odd volunteer from work for the day when he started putting labels on the bottle upside down.

Rook Cutler was with her. Just yesterday, they'd been swept into a dance, right there. One of the old men insisted on pulling out a harmonica on his break, and for five minutes the volunteers all danced, stamping their feet up and down, the bottles jittering in their crates.

'How's it going over there?' my father asked at breakfast in the morning. They had never discussed the idea of his wife working. She fell into it taking Grumps his lunch every day.

Looking around, she saw she could be useful and rolled up her sleeves.

'Not so bad, I'm in charge of orders now. I'm better with the clients. I've more patience for listening to them, I suppose,' she said. 'How's work with you?'

'The same, all waves, weather and delays.'

The cottage was so old the windows distorted the view. It was possible to see ripples in the pane, the glass shifting over the decades. Mum poured coffee and looked out towards the barn where Rook was standing on a ladder, reaching up to the gutters in leather gloves. Clumps of moss squelched in his fists and fell to the ground. The barn door was ajar. Inside we could see a stack of used barrels waiting to be chopped. Outside, Rook scooped moss from the gully and bobbed his blackbird-dark head out of the way of the sodden leaves. He leant back, losing his footing, the ladder wobbling beneath him. He fell with a clank.

'I'll be in tonight at about – ' my father was telling my mother.

'Oh my God!' She dashed out, dressing gown flapping behind her, belt trailing on the grass. 'Rook, Rook, are you alright?' Her voice was an octave higher than we'd ever heard it before. It poured out into the still air and lingered, the crows falling silent.

Rook pulled himself up, staggered and fell. She gripped his hand, attempting to keep him awake. 'What day is it?' she asked. 'What did you have for supper last night? When's my birthday?'

It was just me and my father in the kitchen. He looked on, but didn't join her outside. Just as, last night, he had passed the distillery on his way in, heard music, saw everyone dancing, and lingered in the lane, watching through the window without coming in.

'Sometimes I wonder if anyone would notice if I wasn't here.' He lifted his cup and mumbled into the dregs of his coffee.

'Pardon?' I said.

'Nothing.'

He shrugged on his jacket and left. I didn't tell my mother what I'd heard. I didn't think it mattered. I didn't even mention it when she peered in at the casserole and slammed the oven door at dinner time.

'What's keeping him? Where could he be?' She looked out for my father and grabbed a ladle. 'Well, we'll have to start without him. I can't wait any more. I'm starving. Rook, if you want to stay for something to eat you're welcome, someone should appreciate it.'

I considered telling her what my father told me that morning and thought better of it. It wasn't important. I probably misheard it. I wanted to mishear. I had plans of my own.

The boat churned. I gripped the sides, stomach lurching. It was supposed to be a surprise. We weren't going to the mainland to see *Village of the Damned* after all. There'd be no popcorn and waxy boxes of fruit gums but a picnic on one of the islands. To get there we all had to clamber into Dobby's rowing boat with the motor on board.

'That's where we're going, that island over there, see?' Cal pointed across the water. 'You said you'd never been anywhere.'

Blair looked at her clothes, a spray of water on her sleeve, the lingering smell of fish in the boat crinkling her pretty nose.

'You could have told me, I'd have worn something different.'

It was quiet on the island, other than the screech of terns and the portable radio Dobby had brought. He fetched a blanket and a flask of whisky out of the boat with a grin.

'That's all you brought? No sandwiches? Strawberries? Nothing?' Blair asked. 'What sort of picnic doesn't have any food?'

Dobby pulled her towards him. 'The fun kind.'

'You're crinkling my blouse. Quit it.' Blair made to pull away before accepting his arm around her. 'OK, you're blocking the wind anyway.'

We huddled together, sipping whisky and wandering around looking at the buildings that remained on the island. The cottages had long been abandoned. Some gave the impression someone had left in a hurry, leaving their doors open, the furniture still inside. Pigeons roosted above items that had been left as they were: a bed, a pair of shoes, a table, a colander, a rusted tin of beans on a shelf, a crib covered in a canopy of cobwebs. The boys looked around debating the worth of everything and decided there was nothing they could sell.

'What happened? Why would anyone just abandon the place?'

'The winters, work, illness. The larger islands started getting electricity and shops, people started drifting over.'

'I don't blame them.' Blair wrapped her arms across her chest. 'It's creepy here. It's like a horror film.'

'Don't be stupid,' said Dobby. 'What's going to get you out here? Killer puffins? Seaweed? You're perfectly safe.'

'I'm not scared,' I said. 'They're just buildings. It's sad if anything.'

I wandered on with Cal, Blair and Dobby behind us. Every so often, we heard a light slap. 'Are you an octopus? Keep your hands where I can see them, Squid Boy!' There was one cottage that caught our eye and we wandered towards it. It didn't look quite as derelict as the rest. It had a red door and the cracks in the windows had been taped over with paper.

'I dare you to go in,' Dobby said. I cupped my hands across my face, looking through the cottage window. Whoever had left the place must have dashed off towards cinemas, heated swimming pools and factory work so suddenly they hadn't had time to pack all their clothes. A bag and a man's coat remained hooked to the door.

'Why would I want to go in there?' I asked.

'Because you're not scared, apparently. I dare you to go in, go to the top window and wave at us,' said Dobby.

I walked in on my own, leaving the laughter of my friends behind me. I moved slowly, eyes straight ahead. The stairs groaned beneath me. The sound of a pigeon pattered on the landing roof. The cottage was filthy, littered with paper and bottles. Whoever had left it hadn't been bothered to carry their bedstead downstairs, even though it was brass and someone would have saved up for it once. It would have been a new bride's pride and joy. Yet they had left the bed with a grey blanket and a grubby pillow on the mattress, a pair of reading glasses perched on a newspaper beside it. I headed towards the window and waved, cheering. 'There, I did it! I told you I wasn't scared.' The door opened behind me. I turned. The man stood so close his face was inches away from my own.

'What the fuck do you want?'

He wore braces and a grubby shirt. The stink of cigarettes and stale drink billowed from his mouth. The only clean thing about him was his beard, whiter than washing powder.

'I'm sorry, I didn't know anyone lived here. I thought the island was uninhabited. I was just –'

'Just what?' He stepped closer. The fusty smell of him reminded me of winter, clothes draped over bannisters taking too long to dry. 'Who are you? Where you from?'

'I'm Lorrie, Lorrie Wilson. I just came for a look around. I'm sorry, I'll be out of your way now.' I made for the door. His wrinkled fingers clamped onto my shoulder, holding me back.

'Wait a minute.' He spun me around to face him. 'You've the look of a West girl. From the distillery? You Joseph West's daughter?'

'He's my grandfather,' I said.

'Shit! I should have known. You've got the West nose alright.'

The man turned sideways and tapped the bridge of his nose. I covered my own with my hand, sharp as a ski slope, the same as Grumps' – and the one belonging to the man in front me.

'How is the bastard?' When the old man swore his face was almost gleeful. 'Did he get my messages?'

I gawped, failing to understand. Grumps never wrote letters and he didn't trust phones. Whenever the phone rang at the distillery he would bellow 'What do they want now? There's always something!' He bemoaned the day my mother ever convinced him to have it installed. I never saw him make a single call.

'He's fine,' I said. 'I'll send him your regards.'

'Tell him no such fucking thing. Haven't spoke to him for donkey's years, don't intend to start now. That business of his should have been mine. Our fathers set it up together. And what did my father get? Sweet fuck all.' He spat when he spoke, I winced. It took all my energy not to wipe my face in front of him.

I'd heard the story before. Everyone had. Whenever anyone on the island warned someone about the dangers of gambling they would point to the chimneys in the distance. The brothers who owned the distillery couldn't get along. One worked hard. One had a fondness for women and song. It got to a point of the pair fighting so much they couldn't go on. Since neither could afford to buy the other out, they dragged out a deck of cards and selected one apiece. Whoever drew the lowest card would walk away from the business. A jack and an ace. My great-grandfather won.

'So you must be Abel,' I said.

'Too right.' Abel spat on the floor.

AN EVALUATION OF ABEL WEST

Nose: The whiff of fires he keeps stocked beneath a copper pot, the spirit he distils in a shack drop by drop. The scent of gobstoppers he and my grandfather shared suck for suck as boys is long gone. His father upped and moved off the island with him. There's only the heat of moonshine on his tongue now and a dozen grudges he mutters to himself, lost as the angel's share of the spirit evaporating in the air.

Palate: Roasted bird, chicken, raven, pheasant, plucked and plunged into a sizzling pot. Every meal he cooks lasts for days. There are two kinds of animals alone to him. The ones who bark if anyone approaches your still, and the ones that do nothing for you. Those are for eating.

Finish: Thin as the streams he follows to set up a still in a shack with 'None of Your Business' painted on the door. He has a beard longer than Santa's, hands drier than stone and a face just as hard. There's no shortage of work on the island, but he prefers to be on his own. He'd sooner die than make money for someone else. He'd rather make something than buy it, and sees making moonshine as a right. He regrets little, yet ponders some nights what life could have been, if things had been different and his father hadn't lost the distillery. It could have been his life.

Overall: Looking at him, I see who my grandfather could have been, if his father had lost a bet and set off to live alone in the middle of nowhere. That's the only difference between the men, when it comes down to it: luck. One was lucky in business and love. One never seemed to be in the right place at the right time; it appears imbedded in every line in his face.

'Tell the bastard you saw me,' Abel said.

'It was a pleasure meeting you.'

'No it fucking wasn't.'

I rushed out to the fresh air and my friends. They stared at the old man glowering out of the window, unsure whether to wait for me or run.

'You alright? What happened? Is that Abel West? Shit. I thought he was dead.'

'You know him?'

'Everyone knows him! He's a legend, crazy fucker. Keeps himself to himself, comes to the village every now and then, loads up his boat with supplies, sells some of his moonshine and kicks up a stink.'

Cal slipped his arm around me, oddly impressed. 'You feisty like him?'

I took a mouthful of whisky from his flask, shaking, the dust of the cottage settling in my lungs.

'What do you think?' I laughed until the shaking stopped.

I'm pushing my hands over my ears like I'm crash-landing in an aeroplane or something. The world's spinning. The air's rushing in my ears. I'm falling, and falling, and nothing will ever be the same ever again. *Bam!* It's only paper I can hear but it's deafening. Ma's scrunching the note in her fist and waggling it in my face.

'What's this I found on your shelves?'

I stare at her clutching the picture of a droopy flower and *Would you like to . . .?* The *Definitive Guide to Birds* book I'd sandwiched Joe's note between lies on the bedside table. I have no idea why Ma picked it up. I would have thought she let birdsong wash over her.

'It's nothing. Just a wee thing Joe wrote ages ago. I didn't even reply,' I say.

Ma's mouth keeps moving like a lousy ventriloquist. I stare at her like a busted dummy. The more she keeps talking, the less I can open my mouth. It flaps open and shuts. She's harping on about the problem with lads, and keeping secrets, and how I need to be careful and keep to myself. I count the birds on the wallpaper. One. Two. Three. Four . . . Forty-five. She keeps yammering on and on. There's no one to shush her. Seth and Zach had a hankering to paint the stock room the colour of a pool table and off they went. They're there now, sprucing it up to look like a pub, but with racks of varnish and wrenches all over the walls.

'Is there anything else I should know about?' says Ma.

The drawer rattles. She's jerking it out of the dresser. Raking for love letters, wee notes, whatever I might be hiding from her. The bottom drawer clatters to the floor. Shite. The scrapbook sits on the carpet surrounded by dust bunnies. Ma opens it with a frown. I look around for her cold cream, all ready to hand it to her.

'What's the meaning of this?' She's flick, flick, flicking through photos of folks kissing the Blarney Stone, blue tits dropping food into baby bird mouths, VE Day, Superman and Lois, and Marilyn blowing a kiss over a birthday cake, just wishing a year of her life away.

'It's nothing. They're just pictures,' I say in my head, but the words won't come out. They're all clagged together in a tight ball in my chest. I feel them rise, but they can't find a way to my mouth. They bounce around my head. There's no sound in the room but Ma. And my shame. My shame sounds like paper rain. Ma's ripping up the scrapbook and letting the pieces fall.

When she can rip no more, and bits of paper are snow on the carpet, she sweeps them all into her palm. Stuffing them into her apron pocket, she carts them out to the bin, unable, even when she's furious, to stop herself clearing up as she goes along.

LORRIE

There wasn't a dance floor, yet we found ourselves dancing. The radio stood on the picnic blanket facing the water. Blair jumped up and grabbed Dobby's hand, a song she knew well coming on.

'I'm bored. It's dead here. Dance with me. Please . . .'

Cal and I watched them sway to a slow song and got up to join them, loose with whisky and feeling more able to be close. I danced with his hand on my waist, my ear a whisper from his mouth.

'I can't stand your friend,' he said. 'I almost didn't come on that last date. I didn't want to be set up with someone like her.'

'Someone like what?' I asked.

'You know, the sort who think they're the queen of everything just because they're pretty.'

'You don't like pretty girls?'

'Course I do, but not the ones who know it. Blair's like a movie that looks amazing until someone turns on the volume, then it's all downhill. I wish she'd shut up sometimes.'

I laughed. I don't know why. Who needs a reason? I had whisky and was out with a boy. I could feel him pressed against me, a hardness digging into to my hip. I knew what it was, though we were never taught it at school. I'd heard enough gossip to realise. I was an avid listener to girls in corridors whispering and making scandalised faces after going on a date.

'I'm not seeing him again, I could see his thing in his trousers! Standing up, stiff as a dead snake. We were just sitting on the sofa eating cheese on toast for God's sake! What sort of pervert gets it up for Cheddar?' I pondered every word, memorising it for when I'd need the information.

The song faded. I stepped away from Cal, unsure where to look.

'We're going for a walk,' Dobby wrapped his arm around Blair and she tottered away with him for some time alone. I sat on a rock facing the water, pretending I couldn't hear her giggling behind the abandoned boathouse. 'That tickles,' she said. 'Stop, not that way, my skirt will get grubby.'

Cal sat beside me, slipped his arm around my shoulder and kissed me. We'd kissed once before, so suddenly I hadn't thought about it. He'd reached for me when he dropped me off and I'd let him. The kiss had been smoky and wet. It wasn't unpleasant, but there had been no fireworks either. No shooting stars or flipping in my stomach. Nothing. I'd put it down to being so nervous I could feel nothing else, but this kiss was the same: wet and empty. I jerked away, feeling his fingers sliding over my knee, creeping up my dress.

'No.' I grabbed his hand and placed it on his own leg. Cal looked shocked to see it.

'I want to go,' I said.

'Don't be silly.' He squeezed my shoulder, pulling me closer. 'Not just yet.' He gestured towards the boathouse. 'Your friend's a bit busy, don't be a spoilsport.'

I stood up and called to Blair, 'Can we go now? I'm freezing. I don't want to be late.'

There was no answer. I called louder, 'I want to go. Blair, I'm serious . . .'

'Hang on a minute . . .' Dobby called. I waited on the shale beach, feet crunching on the gravel, my heels digging in.

'I don't know what's wrong with you, we've got loads of time.' Blair came out from behind the boathouse straightening her skirt, clicking open her compact and checking her lipstick. 'You're being a total killjoy.'

We stepped into the boat. I kept my eyes on the mainland, the curve of the coast. The water rippled with light. I clutched the seat under me, the wind whipping around us. I gritted my teeth, determined not to complain.

'What's the matter? You scared of the water? Seasick?' Cal lurched to one side, the boat tilting under him. He lurched to the other.

'Stop it.' I was shaking. 'It's not funny. I can't swim.'

'Relax, it's fine.' Dobby laughed with Cal. There was no danger in anything for them. They knew these waters the way a boy knows how much he can get away with before making his mother cry. I jumped out of the boat before it anchored. The land was only a few feet away, but I couldn't wait. I waded knee-deep through the water with my shoes in my hand.

'Come on! What you doing?' Blair called after me. 'Where you going?'

I ran with their voices following me.

'It was just a joke! We weren't really going to tip the boat. Don't be stupid. Wait and we'll give you a ride. You can't walk all the way.'

I kept running, miles from home, and not caring. I'd die before I went back. I'd rather walk all night than be locked in a car with Dobby at the wheel and Cal at my side.

I passed a deer, or a deer passed me. The stag charged out of the woods and paused a few feet in front of me, breath steaming around its nose. I watched it pause by the roadside, sniff the evening and bolt into the trees. There was nothing here but me, the deer and a light in the distance. I froze in the headlights. The approaching car slowed.

'Lorrie? What you doing out here?' Rook Cutler leant out of the window. I climbed into his van with my shoes in my hand. I could smell the fish he'd been catching. The bottom of my sodden skirt dripped onto one of them, flopped on the floor beside the passenger seat.

'I was out for a walk and lost my direction.' I shivered, rubbing my feet.

Rook twisted out of his jacket and handed it to me. I pulled it over myself. The insides were still warm. He watched me pick grit off the soles of my feet, opened the glove compartment and gave me a flask of water and a cloth. I sipped the water. Dabbing some on the cloth, I wiped my face.

'You're freezing,' he said. 'My place isn't far. We'll stop there, then I'll take you home.'

'No, it's alright, I'm fine.' I spotted myself in the rear-view, streaks of mascara on my face and lipstick smudged around my mouth. I was already late.

'I was just – '

'I don't have to know what you've been up to.' Rook held up a hand the way a policeman stops traffic. I didn't say more. He was right. It wasn't far to his. He lived in one of a pair of cottages on their own near the loch. I followed him in.

'Come in, get yourself dry.' I sat by the fire, the embers crackling. He threw on another log. I stretched out my legs to let my skirt dry, pulled off my stockings and stuffed them in my bag. Rook looked away. He didn't sit with me. Looking around, he couldn't if he wanted to. There was only one armchair. There was only one of everything. One chair. One fire. One bowl. One plate and cup on the dresser. One small table. One hunting knife and a breadboard.

'You want something to drink?' he asked.

He looked relieved when I shook my head. He wouldn't have known what to give me. There wasn't enough china to join me.

'It's nice in here,' I said. 'Simple.'

Rook looked around his house. 'It'll do me, anyway. I don't get a lot of company. It's just me and the dog.' The greyhound slept under the table, jaw flat to the ground.

'How come you're not married?' I said. It probably sounded rude, but I couldn't stop myself asking. I was itching to know.

'I don't know. I never met anyone I preferred to my own company, I suppose. Or, maybe I did once, but it was the wrong time.'

'You and my mother go back a long way, yeah?'

'Aye.'

The fire spat a cinder onto the rug. It glowed and paled under his boot stamping it out. Every so often, I'd think about this, years later I'd still regret not asking more during my one time alone with Rook Cutler. I didn't quite know what to ask or how to. I wasn't sure what I should know.

'I found a photo of you and her once,' I said. 'When you were younger. You had my mother on your shoulders, giving her a piggyback. You looked happy. Were you her boyfriend or something?'

'Not really.'

'Why not? Didn't you like her?'

'I did, but I didn't like myself much. I was too selfish to be anybody's boyfriend back then. There's no story to it, I just wasn't ready yet.' Rook repositioned the fireguard. 'That skirt looks dry enough now. Come on, I'll drive you home.'

He pulled his keys out of his pocket and I followed him out. I'd have loved to know more, but he didn't speak any more.

I had other concerns. I was late and I had to figure out a lie about why. It had better be good.

The lights of the house blazed as if someone was afraid of the dark. I got out of the van, certain Rook would follow me and speak to my parents in that low adult voice I'd come to hate: *I found her out on the south side of the island. I think she's been drinking. Lipstick all over the place, wet skirt, filthy feet.*

Rook didn't get out the car. He waited in the lane until I reached the door and pulled away. Occasionally, afterwards, I'd see him at the distillery and nod. Adult or not, if he suspected I'd been up to no good he never breathed a word.

'That you Lorrie? You in?' my mother called to the click of the door.

I looked at myself in the mirror. In the light of hall, my attempt to wash my face didn't look as convincing as it had felt in the moonlight. I poked my head around the door without going into the lounge.

'It's just me.'

Grumps was asleep in his chair, one hand moving, swatting the flies of his dreams. Toby was already in bed. My mother was doing nothing but waiting.

'I've been listening out for your father,' she said. 'He never came in from work. When I phoned, they said he didn't show up this morning.'

I waffled my excuses about being late, but she was only half listening. One ear was fixed on outside, waiting for the sound of my father's brogues on the path.

'Blair's mother dropped me off along the lane,' I said.

'Can she drive OK?' My mother knitted her fingers together. 'With one hand, I mean.'

'She can. They gave her an artificial hand with a driving glove on it.' I was aware of her inspecting my face, noticing my smudged lipstick and streaks of mascara on my cheek. 'Blair gave me a makeover,' I said. 'And to think she wants to work at a beauty counter in a department store in the city. She'd be better off doing horror films. I look like Vampira.'

I was back to knowing what to say, even if it wasn't the truth. I didn't want the sandwich my mother offered me, or the cocoa. I wanted only my bed and the day to be over with.

I brushed the aftertaste of cigarettes and spirits out of my mouth. Courting made me think of swimming lessons. I had dived into the deep end. I wanted someone who would make me feel I was floating but could still put my feet on the bottom of the pool. Gripping my toothbrush, I looked out towards Zach's bedroom. The lamp was lit in Sylvie's room. I saw a flicker of curtain and her light going out. It reminded me of my mother leaving all the lights on until everyone was here. I wondered if Sylvie had been waiting to see if I'd got in OK, if she'd have been up all night, if I'd been the one who never made it home.

There's loads and loads of stuff to do when you're grounded. It doesn't bother me that much. It used to be worse before Seth came and Ma could lock me in. Just knowing there was a key in the other side of the door bugged me, but I kinda like my room. I can spend ages and ages just staring at stuff and wondering. I stare at the wallpaper and think the scrolly pattern between the birds kinda looks like someone water-skiing. It's a wee thing I noticed once while Ma was nagging. I was about six. It was only discovering the secret life in the wallpaper that had stopped me crying. Sometimes it's only the small things I find for myself that make sense. I asked Lorrie once what she thought the shapes on the wallpaper looked like, and she said 'just swirls'. I suppose normal people don't stare at everything and find other worlds. Sometimes I think I'd love to be like everyone else, just to fit in. But sometimes I think I'd miss the wonders of wallpaper. I don't hate that part of myself.

Ma wants me to spend time reading the Bible, chipping in with the housework, and thinking about what I've done. I wander about the place like a hound dog, all droopy-eyed and fearty looking. It's the only way to keep her happy.

Seth's sitting with her in the kitchen. They don't hear me and start gabbling about mashed potato as soon as they see me, but it's too late. I've heard everything.

'What you punishing the lass for this time? You're too hard on her,' Seth says.

'I dislike her attitude,' says Ma.

'She seems alright to me, always got her head in a book,' Seth says. 'She's not fighting, or swearing, or stealing. It could be worse.'

'She could be better,' Ma says. 'But she won't be, unless I lay down the law. You don't know her. Give her an inch . . .'

Seth shrugs. He's done all he can. He can't push it, or she might start griping at him to quit playing cards again.

'Jesus, lass!' He notices me and jumps out of his skin like he just saw a ghost with a duster. 'I didn't see you there! You're a wee creeping Jesus! Don't be scared to make a sound, lass, and let folks know you're here! Come in, we were just trying to decide what to have for tea.'

Seth's smiling. Ma's not. I stay where I am in the doorway. Not quite able to come in and join them, and having nowhere else to go neither.

LORRIE

Miss Stone stood at the front of the class, arching her fingers. 'Today, most of you will be ready for buttonholes.' She glanced at Marge. The girls giggled at the upholsterer's daughter picking her blistered fingertips. I didn't join in. I was waiting for Blair to breeze in late, smelling of Juicy Fruit, cigarettes and excuses. She wouldn't be happy at the way we'd left things at the weekend. I'd been a baby, dashing off the way I had. I was no fun. I'd agree rather than get into a fight with her. I couldn't explain why I had to get away from there. It had nothing to do with logic and everything to do with a shiver running through me, standing by the water, sitting in that boat beside Cal. I could think nothing but: I have no control, I don't want to rely on these people to get home.

The headmaster waved through the porthole in the classroom door. Miss Stone joined him in the corridor and I watched their faces through the small window. Miss Stone tugged her bottom lip, shaking her head. The headmaster placed his hand on her shoulder.

'Blair Munro won't be joining us today.' Miss Stone cleared her throat, addressing the class. 'We've been informed she was involved in an accident and is in hospital. Perhaps the class could embroider a card for her? It would be lovely for her to see we're thinking of her.'

I raised my hand. 'What sort of accident? When did it happen? Where?'

'It was at the weekend. I'm afraid I don't have all the details.' Miss Stone strolled around the room, a waft of coffee and perfume passing over our shoulders as she inspected our sewing. I dug Blair's nightdress out of my bag and laid it on the workbench. I hadn't done the tacking she'd asked me to finish for her, claiming her nails were too long to hold a needle, but I would. Miss Stone lay a palm on the nightdress. Gauzy, cerise, light as a cancan dancer.

'I want to finish it for her,' I said. I waited for the teacher to suggest, 'Perhaps she'd rather complete it herself when she comes back,' but she didn't.

'That would be a kind thing to do,' she said.

I pinned lace to the nightdress and stared at my fingers under the fabric. I pictured a girl falling into a loch, floating in moonlight brighter than smashed glass. I shouldn't have left her on her own. Whatever happened was my fault. No, that was crazy. I wasn't God, just a friend. When I was sixteen, the two felt the same.

It would just be a bump on the head, a scuff here, a graze there. I was sure. The hospital was a long Victorian building. I went in expecting the worst and found Blair in a room on her own. She lay in bed, her red hair making comma shapes on the pillow. Her eyes were closed and her face looked scrubbed clean. Without her make-up, she looked so young I'd have walked past her on the street. I searched the crisp sheets across her for any sign of broken bones and could see nothing wrong. The only mark on her was a dark bruise on her forehead, small as a thumbprint.

'Hello.' My voice echoed through the room. I lowered it. Blair didn't move. 'Well, you don't have to sew that nightdress now anyway. Miss Stone said I can finish it for you. Honestly, the stuff you'll pull to get out of sewing.' I laughed to crack the silence wide open. I'd never seen her so still. I clawed through my bag, laid the nightdress on the bed and arranged it over her sleeping body. It looked ready for Blair to push off the covers, flounce into it and laugh. I stretched the measuring tape across her blanket-covered ankles and began pinning the hem to the correct length. I turned, alerted by the sound of someone trying to walk quietly on the tiled floor. Mrs Munro entered with a man struggling with the straightness of his tie.

'Lorrie, isn't it?' she asked. 'So sweet of you to come to see Blair.' Mrs Munro was wearing a suit. Everything about her was crisp as a hospital corner. She bore no resemblance to the woman I'd seen dancing barefoot in her lounge.

'Did you bring this?' She touched the nightdress covering Blair.

'I'm finishing it for her.'

'She'd love that,' Mrs Munro said. 'She will love it when she wakes up. They're not sure when, but . . .' The man placed a hand on her shoulder. He'd never let her stumble, even for words. 'Oh, I didn't introduce you. This is Ned, a friend of mine. This is Lorrie, Blair's friend.'

Ned shook my hand and folded a business card into it in the same gesture. The rectangle of paper had a picture of a vacuum cleaner with eyes and lips sucking up bubbles. Carpet cleaner guy. Mrs Munro's date must have gone better than ours.

'Really, Ned! What's she going to do with carpet cleaning? She's just a slip of a girl!'

'Sorry, it's a habit.' Ned cleared his throat. 'I shake so many hands all day. Hey, but if your parents need a carpet cleaning sometime let me know. Any friend of Blair's . . .'

Mrs Munro patted his arm.

'Ned's been a rock during all this. I can't wait for Blair to meet him.' The three of us stared at the girl, united by her silence, each of us imagining she'd hear us talking about her and leap out of bed.

'You were with her on Friday, weren't you?' Mrs Munro asked.

'We met some friends for a bit, then I had to go,' I said. 'What happened?'

'I'm not sure. The lad driving her hit a deer and came off the road. He's fine, so was Blair, just a wee bump on her head. She came in, drank some water and went straight to bed. In the morning, I couldn't wake her up.'

I wondered if it was the same deer I had seen and why it mattered, why I felt I had to know.

'There's just one thing I have to ask, Lorrie, was anyone drinking or anything? Was that why it happened? Blair never introduced me to the lad she was out with, so I can't ask.'

'I don't think so. I didn't see anything like that.' I stuffed the nightdress into my bag and swung it over my shoulder. 'I have to be going, my parents are expecting me.' I rushed to the door.

I didn't know if Blair would want me to tell her mother what we'd been doing. She was nothing like the woman I'd seen draped over the jukebox. That was the sort of woman I might have told, not this one. This one reminded me of my parents and their *I'm not angry, I just expected more from you* look. It was better to say nothing while Blair was sleeping, I decided. I didn't want her to wake up and be furious at me for me for getting her boyfriend in trouble. Nor did I want where I was getting back to my mother. She had enough to worry about with my father. That morning, Toby and I had left for school with apples, a peck on our cheeks and instructions to have a lovely day while she went to the police station to report a missing person.

I'm wandering along carrying the milk when I bump into the lad. Ma's making rice pudding, so she makes me pop down to the honesty box down the lane for goat's milk. The sign over the box says *Farm Fresh Eggs, Milk, & Potatoes*. It's my favourite sign on the island because underneath they've wrote: *Come, help yourself!* The writing has rounded happy looking letters like the farmer still remembers being a wee lad learning his ABCs. I pop my coins in the slot and spot the lad outside the gate, right near our own box full of our eggs. He's shuffling around with his hands in his pockets, a bear in a cage. Pacing.

'Where's Lorrie?' he says. 'She lives here, right?'

'She went off somewhere after school,' I say. 'Said she had something to do.'

I haven't got a clue what she's up to. All she told me was to tell her mother she had to go to the library or something. And then she was off, flitting towards town.

Just looking at the lad, I know who he is. This is him. The date. The one I saw kiss her. He kinda looks like he's got a pocket full of centipedes. Wriggly jiggly. He bites his lip and scrapes his thumbnail on his sharp little teeth. He looks way too fidgety to stand still and put his arms around anyone.

'You're her pal, right? I've seen you kicking around with her. When will she be back?'

I shrug. He steps closer. I step back. The milk wobbles in the bottle.

'Tell her I'm looking for her. It's urgent,' he says.

I spin around and call after him wandering away. I can hear his pockets jangling.

'Who should I say was asking after her?' I yell.

'Cal. Tell her Cal has to see her. Big time. She'll know who you mean.'

I'm making my way into the house, then I turn back. I lift the lid of our honesty box. There's not one coin in there, though the eggs have all sold. I knew there was something fishy about him. Twitchy. I wonder why Lorrie went out with him and why he's gagging to see her. It must have been a hell of a date.

LORRIE

I lay on my bed wishing I had a radio to drown out the hush of the house. It was so quiet, I could hear the voice of my mother telling Toby everything would be fine. There must be a reason Dad hadn't come home. He'd never stayed out a single night before, let alone four. There had to be an explanation. Knowing him it would be so mundane we wouldn't be able to stop ourselves yawning.

I rubbed my temples in circles, picturing Blair lying in bed, the silvery blue of her eyelids clenched, a flicker of movement beneath. Grumps knocked on my door, poked his head around it and came in with a shot glass of whisky and honey.

'This will help your cold,' he said. 'Just a bit, drink it slowly.'

I'd told everyone I thought I was getting a cold as an excuse to get away. I sniffed to prove I was sick and accepted the whisky. Grumps narrowed his eyes, discerning I was putting it on. He always knew more than he let on.

'You'll drift off in no time. Everything may not be alright tomorrow, but it always looks better when you've had your sleep.'

He perched on a wicker chair, unable to bring himself to sit on a pink bedspread. It wasn't often I was alone with my grandfather. Our conversations usually involved appraisals of the weather and my mother's porridge-making skills, but I was glad he was here. It was a relief to have the sort of company that didn't require much of me.

'Tell me a story. It will help me get to sleep,' I said. I realised I was too old for stories, but I'd pretend I wasn't, just once. Tonight, I'd have some time off from being an adult.

'I don't know any stories,' Grumps said. This was the beginning of the story, always. *I don't know any stories* was his Once Upon a Time.

'Tell me how you met Grandma.'

'You already know.'

'I don't know how you'll tell it tonight,' I replied.

Grumps picked a toothpick out of his pocket and poked around his mouth for leftover lunch and scraps of memory.

'She worked at the bakery. Seventeen, shy, and prettier than a piglet in April, but she was the most serious girl I ever saw.'

I settled into my pillow and waited. This was the only story he ever told me. He was always happy to tell it, so long as I coaxed it out of him.

'Every day, I'd see her through the window kneading bread, concentrating, biting her lip, but I never asked her out. I just kept going in, buying loaves. I had so many loaves I would toss chunks of bread out the window every night. It looked like it had snowed. The grass outside would be covered in birds.'

'You could have asked her to go out with you,' I said.

'I couldn't. Some things are out of a person's league. It's best to recognise what they are and avoid disappointment. I wasn't always as handsome as I am now, you know.' Grumps grinned a flash of grey tooth and bunched his lips.

'One night, nature was on my side, a storm hit the island. The wind was fearsome. Thunder and lightning clattered like a cutlery drawer. There were so many trees in the road the passing places became unpassable. One tree crashed through her aunt's roof. I was working as a roofer for Ed Campbell that year, to tide myself over until my father said I was old enough to work at the distillery. I had a head for heights, but talking to the ladies made me dizzy. That's the only thing that made me feel I might fall. I suppose Ed saw I was shy, so he stuck his oar in. "If you'll go out with Joseph this Saturday," he said to your grandmother, "I'll give your aunt a few quid off fixing her slates." Cheeky swine. Maisy folded her arms and stared at me for a long time. "Make it five," she said, "then we'll talk." That was it, a fiver for a lifetime. I was working at the distillery a year later, soon as I turned eighteen. We got married not long after that.'

In silence, we separately recalled my grandmother – a bolster of a woman stuffed with phrases such as: *wash your hands before you dig in*; *well, if wishes were fishes*; *there's no point crying about it now*. My parents had visited every New Year before we moved to the island. I always found her in the kitchen waiting for the first foot in, just where she had been when I had left. She gave the impression she hadn't moved since, holding the kettle in her hands or moving her knife between a pie and tin, sliding out pastry without making a break. The repertoire of her conversations consisted of: *there's plenty more if you want it . . .* ; *you look like your mother, but thicker*; *you look like your father*. She'd glance at Toby and cut him more cake to compensate. Grumps never took his eyes off her. He would sit quietly as his daughter and wife chatted about the journey, who'd died on the island, who married who and who was still single. Grandma would stop talking and turn to him suddenly, aware of him looking at her.

'Soppy old fool,' she would say, though we couldn't spot him smiling. It seemed as though they'd been having a conversation no one else in the room could hear. They had been. It was conversation of eyes and years only they could understand.

I closed my eyes as Grumps left, whispering, 'Sleep tight, don't let the bedbugs . . .'

I heard no more, out for the night.

1ST JUNE 1960

It's not like Ma suddenly trusts me, or Lorrie's become some kinda saint overnight. It's Lorrie's father that's stopping her keeping me grounded. Being missing changes everything. Ma says I can pop over and keep Lorrie company. It's the Christian thing to do. I carry a bannock on her behalf.

Lorrie's ma is a rhubarb jelly machine. Steam's crying down the windows. She's darting about the kitchen sticking labels to squeaky-clean jars like she's bottling bits of her heart.

'Hey there, Sylvie,' she says. 'How you doing? It's been a while.'

'I know. I've had a lot of schoolwork.'

Honestly, I've had no more than Lorrie, but I can't exactly tell her about the note off Joe and Ma raging. What goes on within these walls is private, Ma says. Tell nothing to no one. It's the law.

The tree outside Lorrie's room is making crazy shadows like wallpaper that won't stay still. Lorrie puts the radio on instead of blethering. There's nothing anyone's saying about her pa we want to repeat. Folks in the village have stopped saying he must have a flat tyre or something. They've given him a fancy woman instead. They reckon he's shacked up with some floozy he's had on the side for years. They're so convinced it's true they can practically see her standing around in a silk slip. Looking over his shoulder, just outside of the picture Rook Cutler's been posting all over telephone poles on the mainland.

'I can't stand the waiting,' Lorrie says. 'Not knowing.'

Toby bursts into the room clutching a rope in his hand. 'Tie me up as tight you can,' he says. 'I want to see if I can escape.'

'Toby! What have I told you about knocking?' Lorrie snaps.

'If I knock you'll tell me to get knotted.' He's all pimples and hair like a duck's arse and an energy that won't let him sit still. 'Go on, tie me up,' he says. 'Tight.'

'Piss off and bug someone else.'

'I can't. Mum's gone jam crazy and Grumps has gone fishing.'

He holds his fists out in front of him, dangling the rope. I grab it and wind it around his wrists. Toby sits on the floor, knees bent. 'Now do my ankles,' he says. I wind the rope because Lorrie won't. It's always been this way with Toby and me. When Lorrie's not bothering with either of us, he'll catch me in the garden sometimes and get me to pick a card. Or I'll stand over him with a stopwatch, timing how long it takes him to get out of a barrel with his hands tied.

'Tighter.' He wriggles and writhes and gets nowhere. 'Now watch me get out.'

The knot remains firm.

'I don't have time for this,' Lorrie says. 'Get out. Now. Hop it!' She hurls the pin cushion at him and he squirms out the door fast as a wee caterpillar, still on the floor.

'You didn't have to shout at him,' I say. I reckon all he's after is escaping wondering where his pa is, but I don't say. Lorrie's got her head in her hands.

'I have to finish this for Blair,' she says. And she picks up the nightdress sprawled on the chair. She lays it across her lap like a lassie who turned into air. *Pouf!* I kinda want to put my arm around her and say something comforting, but I can't get the words out. I start picking dropped pins off the floor.

'Your collar's all wonky,' I say.

'Eh?'

'On your nightdress. Look at the trim. It's wobbly as fuck.' I snatch the scissors and set about unpicking stitches. I don't know if Lorrie's father will come home. Or when Blair will wake up. I can't tell her nothing, but I can sew. I'll sew a lace frill for a bonnie lassie I hate. And I'll do it for Lorrie. I don't want to do more, but I could, if I have to, for my pal.

PART III

LORRIE

There was a quiet spot Sylvie loved to go for the puffins. We spotted them congregating out near the lighthouse and she'd drag me to see the birds. Oddly, she never had a problem speaking when we were sitting on those rocks, looking out at flashes of red across the waves. It was possible for her to spend an hour quite happily doing nothing but looking. It was the site of one of our favourite childhood conversations on days where nothing happened but the weather. *Who do you wish would show up now? If anything could happen, what would you pick?* I'd always opt for Dean Martin arriving in a sports car. Sylvie looked up and wondered about it raining frogs. Or, out of nowhere, she'd say, 'Imagine if a squid crawled out of the water over there, a giant one, that would liven things up a bit.' Her eyes would sparkle with thoughts of fishermen battling a kraken. She would grin, certain the beady-eyed woman from the newsagent would rush out to wrestle the monster, convinced it was coming to nick her liquorice. Today, Sylvie wondered what would happen if the puffins suddenly started talking, not just the puffins but every bird on the island. They'd have plenty to say.

'Look at their stubby wings going like the clappers. They look too daft to be able to fly, but they can,' she said. 'It's a shame they don't come as close as when they were just out of the nest. I don't blame them though. Ha ha, look at that one gobbling the fish!'

I glanced at the bird she'd been pointing at. I was grateful for the distraction. The police were searching for my father, plodding about with Alsatians with their noses in the bracken. I couldn't stand the thought of it. Nor could I stand being at home. The house was brittle with waiting, the slightest cough or creak in the floorboards made us flinch. My mother put the radio on quieter than normal. Toby kept his bedroom door open. Everyone was tiptoeing around pretending not to be waiting to hear something, all of us picturing the same things we'd never admit out loud.

The air nipped our fingers. Sylvie and I plunged our hands into our pockets, turned our backs on the lighthouse and made our way to the harbour. The clouds were rolling inland. The shopkeepers were braced for a storm. We turned into the cobbled square, wondering whether to wait for the bus, or chance walking and being caught by a storm.

'I'm all out of sour plums,' Sylvie said. 'I'll just pop in and get some, do you want anything?' I shook my head and she entered the newsagents. I looked in at glass jars full of boiled sweets stacked floor to ceiling, and dawdled along the street to the hardware store.

There was a red wheelbarrow in the window. I looked across it to the rear of the store where Zach was sealing a lid on a paint tin. I pictured buying the shiny wheelbarrow the way some say it with flowers. Zach and I never spoke about how we felt about anything, but we could speak the language of hardware. Sylvie once told me he considered the red wheelbarrow a beautiful thing. He hoped to own one just like it some day when he had his own place.

I saw the face in the window before I could turn around.

'Hello beautiful. Have you missed me?' Cal grabbed me from behind. There was a graze on his cheek. It suited him. Some faces look right with glasses or a suntan, for Cal it was a cut that made him complete. I hadn't scrawled *Lorrie loves Cal* on my notebooks. I hadn't thought of him whatsoever since our date.

'The police have been sniffing about asking about the accident,' he said. 'We have to get our story straight.'

'I won't tell them anything,' I said. 'I wasn't there as far as my parents are concerned.'

'You were there, though. If anyone asks, tell them we weren't drinking, at least.' Cal gripped my arm. He was standing so close behind me I couldn't turn around. A woman came out the chemist pushing a pram and Cal smiled at her, looping his arm around my waist. I stared at our reflections in the window in front of us. We were standing so close we resembled a couple plotting our happy ending. Anyone looking in our direction would assume that's what we were.

'You're selfish.' Cal's smile tightened. 'You could make it easier for all of us,' he said. 'All you care about is yourself.'

Zach glanced our way, prying open a tin of emulsion for a plain woman flicking her hair over her shoulder. He looked away, giving her his complete attention. Cal's arm remained squeezed around me. There was nothing I could do. If I lurched away someone in the street would ask if I was OK. Yet I didn't, I couldn't move.

Cal continued holding me firm, his fingers digging into my ribs. He kissed my neck and whispered, 'If anyone asks, say we weren't drinking, or I'll tell everyone we went all the way.'

'But we didn't – '

'How are you going to prove it?'

'How are you going to prove we did?' I said.

Cal laughed, 'I won't be expected to, that's just how it is.'

I despised him, but he was right. The island would believe any rumour he spread. Even if they weren't completely convinced, it wouldn't matter. People would look at me and wonder.

Everything I wore, said, or did, would call into question my innocence.

Sylvie came out of the store putting up her umbrella. The rain was so fine no one could see it, only feel it, but Sylvie always carried an umbrella, even though she never styled her hair. She came over and stepped to one side, making way for me. I pulled away from Cal more violently than I'd intended. My mother didn't know where I'd been. I intended to keep it that way.

'See you around, ladies.' Cal waved at us huddling beneath the umbrella.

'That's the guy I saw at your gate,' said Sylvie. 'Are you courting?'

'Not really, not any more.' She didn't quiz me for more information. I was grateful.

'You're a good friend,' I said.

Sylvie looked unsure what she'd done to deserve it. I couldn't explain. She was here with her pea-green umbrella dotted with rain. She was simple. She was reliable. She was Sylvie. We plodded on, passing the small swing park just outside the village.

'That's where Mrs Campbell saved my life when I was little,' Sylvie said. 'She wasn't Mrs Campbell then though. It was before Fraser Campbell met her at the fair, so she was just Bonnie Sales then, walking along with her groceries.'

'What happened?'

I couldn't picture Sylvie not looking both ways before she crossed, not even as a child. I couldn't picture Bunny not keeping her on a leash. We followed the winding road, a delivery van charging past at a speed only visitors took on blind bends.

'It was just like that.' Sylvie pointed at the road. 'Someone almost knocked me down and she saved me.'

'How?' I asked.

'I'm not sure. I just know she saved me.'

Sylvie offered me a sour plum and popped one in her mouth. I knew I would get no more out of her and it was fine. There was plenty I didn't want to talk about myself.

THE DAY I LEFT THE SANDPIT

Lorrie wasn't here the day I wandered out the sandpit. I keep trying to remember just how it went, and it's fuzzy. The day feels like something that has been in my pocket forever and has got all woolly with lint. The way I remember it is kinda like this . . .

Ma leaves me in the park while she pops off to do her messages. Off she goes, flitting to some sort of kitchen emergency over the road. I can't remember just what the emergency is. It might be a bride who just moved into a place with a cherry tree and is dying for a stone pitter. Or a wife with so many apples she needs something that peels and cores at the same time. Or some lassie forced to suddenly make forty sandwiches for her stepdad's wake. In any case, Ma's got to save them with gadgets and plastic boxes to stop all their tattie scones going stale. She's leaving me with a spade and strict instructions to stay in the sandpit. I have to promise I'll speak to no strangers. And not wander off into the street.

I have this wee bucket I'm filling with sand. Pouring it out, and filling it up, over and again. The sand's too dry to make a castle. I sit in the pit just looking at the shape my hands make in the sand. There's a wee lad not that far away staring at some kids playing rounders. The steel on his legs sparkles in the sunlight. The shiny metal looks like a cage.

'What's wrong with you?' I say.

I've seen him before. Always in the same place, knuckles white, clutching the wee guitar his ma makes him take everywhere. He plucks it. The kids bounce their balls.

'I had polio,' he says.

I'm so wee I'm not sure what that is, but it doesn't sound fun. I wonder if it means no one will throw him a ball. I look at him and his sulky little mouth that looks like it's never tried smiling. I want it to learn. I want us to be pals. I clamber out of the sandbox and kiss him. Just as he's opening his gob about to say something, that's when I do it. I squish my mouth to his so I won't see it looking sulky any more. I half close my eyes and see my own eyelashes catching the sunlight. Then I pull away.

The wee lad drops his guitar. He looks sorta dozy, just staring at me, his mouth catching flies. He stays that way until his ma calls him to the ice-cream van.

'Joe? Come on, I've got ice lollies!' Sticky orange juice runs down her hands.

The lad hurries towards her without looking back. And everything's swimming. The swings, the sandpit, the bit of cat poo in the corner, the path under my feet, the lady wandering along with a straw bag full of groceries, the cars on the road. I can see Ma leaving someone's house across the street. Tucking change into her purse, skipping down the steps. I'm so dizzy and sick. My legs feel so heavy it feels like I'm plodging through treacle. There's a taste in my mouth fuzzy as green mould. And I want my Ma to make it all better. I stumble towards her. One step, then another, across the street. *Bam!* I'm swept off my feet. The lady with the shopping is swooping in and dragging me off the road. The delivery van blares past honking its horn. Ma's rushing across the street. The groceries are all over the concrete. Tins of peas roll on the path. The eggs are all smashed. The lady's standing over me asking 'Are you OK? Jesus, are you are OK? That came out of nowhere. It missed you by an inch!' I squint at her. My eyes are so heavy and everything's so bright the light is a brass weight forcing them shut. I don't remember any more. I only know it's the last time I'm allowed in the sandpit.

It's the only time I kissed a boy, or someone saved my life. It's also the first time I reckon I really knew something I'd been wondering for a while.

LORRIE

The search came up drier than the laughter of the men in the hardware store. There was more water on the island than hours, more mountains than men. A man could be anywhere out there and no one would know until he washed in. I dawdled in the hardware store on Saturday, staring at Zach at his counter and wishing I could convey what I was thinking with a look. 'That guy you saw me with is nothing to me. He's a practice guy until I can go out with you,' is what I wanted to tell him but, of course, I told him nothing. I fingered the brass hooks and listened to customers gossiping.

'Did they find anything in the loch?' one man asked.

'Tyres. Oilcans. Boots, I saw boot after boot being dragged out the water. They weren't his it turned out, when they showed his wife.'

I knew the police showed some of the things they'd found to my mother. I heard her and Grumps speak about it in hushed tones.

'They found a watch, but it wasn't his, and boots – so many. I wonder who owned them?' she said. 'Did all those men drown?'

It didn't seem likely. The island was the sort of place where if anyone were to drown it wouldn't be long until it became legendary. It would turn into a whisper about phantoms in the mist, a story of the spirits of wives dragging faithless men to their deaths.

'I doubt it,' Grumps said. 'Some fella probably got sick of them pinching his feet, kicked them off and said "fuck this".'

He wanted to make her laugh and it worked, laughter found its way to the surface of her. When she fell quiet again, I could still hear it in the air.

The customers in the hardware store offered no theories about why there were boots in the lake. They were more interested in the last time anyone in the store had seen my father.

'He came in the day before he disappeared, you know. He wandered up to the counter, laid down his wallet and asked, "What will it take to get in on that card game of yours? Cash? How much? Take it. I don't care."'

'No way!' Seth's customers leant forward.

'That's what the man said, word for word. I didn't take him up on it. I don't know the man well enough to play cards with him. There was something off about it.'

I dropped a coat hook. Seth cleared his throat, directing his customers my way. They coughed and looked at the ceiling. I left without buying anything, though I didn't want to go yet. My mother would be clearing out the kitchen cupboards, scrubbing her worries away. Toby would be practising escapology. Bunny had dragged Sylvie to a lecture about ladylike manners at The Island Mothers' meeting. There was nothing for it but to kill time in the chemist, sampling stubby lipsticks and comparing home perm kits. One of my classmates, Marjorie, had recently bought one. It gave her curls so tight everyone called her a sheepie.

Mrs Munro was standing at the lipstick display drawing slashes on the back of her hand.

'Lorrie, hello! Help me.' She waved a lipstick. 'What do you think? Too lurid for a woman my age? Can I get away with it?'

'You can get away with anything you want,' I said.

She smiled and squeezed my arm. She was so pleased to see me it was painful.

AN EVALUATION OF MRS MUNRO

Nose: Her favourite scents are the kohl she dots onto a freckle above her top lip each morning, and the crisp sheets she wafts onto beds in the hotel where she works, barely making a footprint on the carpet after the guests have left. The coins they stack on the dresser with requests for more soap smell like blood to her. They jangle in her overcoat as she pushes the toiletries cart to another door, another floor, the copper growing heavier by the hour.

Palate: The chocolate mints she lays on pillows and stuffs in her pocket are a perk of the job she scatters around her lounge. She bites into the chocolate, then tastes the end of her pen, writing to the court for the maintenance not sent. There's a waxy flavour to the lipstick she paints on. She puts it on slowly, covering her mutters of 'men are all the same', getting the sentiment out of her system before she puts on a love song, sweeps on rouge, and leaves for a late supper with men who are widowed, still single, or just bored.

Finish: Capri pants and pumps that can be kicked off at the end of the day in the manner of a girl who wants to dance, or a woman with blisters on her soles. She is both. In the chemist her face flickers from worry to hope, swinging between the two. She carries the air of a woman grieving and falling in love at the same time. It's the strangest thing I ever saw.

Overall: The mother of my friend, a woman with a demeanour that makes me feel, the more I see it, that if she were twenty years younger it would be her who'd be my friend, rather than her daughter.

I was the closest thing to having a conversation with her daughter she had. Mrs Munro latched on to my presence. The more she spoke, the more I became aware of it.

'You remember Mr . . . Ned,' she said. 'You met him. Yes, carpet cleaner guy! He's introducing me to his parents in Moray. I want to make a good impression.'

'Then I'd go with this one. It's subtler.' I put down a lipstick called Vixen and picked up a shade that made me think of tinned peaches and Carnation.

'You're a star. Have you been to visit Blair lately?'

I hadn't. I hadn't seen her since I bumped into her mother last time.

'That's OK.' Mrs Munro wiped lipstick off her hand. 'They don't know if she can hear us. I visit and just read to her.' She gestured to the romance novel jutting out of her handbag. It had a picture of a highwayman and a woman in a corset on the cover. It was the sort of thing I used to smuggle around to Sylvie's, laughing at the love scenes.

'I only read the highlights, of course. That's all Blair would be interested in.'

Mrs Munro smiled. When she spoke about her daughter her face forgot her age. When she stopped talking, it remembered it again within seconds.

'They're starting to say she may not wake up. They're not sure why, a fracture on her skull in the wrong place. I don't believe them,' she said. 'Blair will wake up, I can feel it in my bones. A mother knows these things.'

Mrs Munro held a finger to her eyes, making a wall between her tears and her powder. The lipstick samples on her hand left an oily stripe on her cheek.

'I'm so sorry,' I said.

'You don't have to be sorry about anything, Lorrie. Doctors get it wrong it all the time. The leaving dance is coming up, right? That's all you should be worrying about at your age.'

Mrs Munro was sixteen again, or, at least doing her utmost to be. She asked what I'd wear and if there was anyone special

I wanted to go with. I found myself describing Zach, though I wasn't sure if I was going to the dance. He hadn't asked. No one had.

'There's one guy,' I said. 'A quiet one. The sort whose idea of heaven is a cold beer, a pot of paint and a long weekend. I never know what he's thinking, but, I don't know.' I shivered. 'He looks at you and your toes curl.'

'Oh, those guys! I've known one or two of those in my time,' Mrs Munro said.

I joined her in a moment of silence for toe-curling guys.

'Well, I suppose I should be going.' She put down all the lipsticks but one. 'I'm meeting Ned. Are you sure this is OK? I want his parents to like me!'

'What's not to like?' Her clothes, her air, her divorce, I saw them all flit across her face. 'If you want someone to like you, all you have to do is say what they want to hear. Compliments, that sort of thing,' I said.

'Oh, Lorrie! If only you knew, it's not that simple to make someone like you!'

'Yes, it is. It's as simple as you want it to be.'

Mrs Munro made her purchase and left, saying she hoped I was right, and, if I was, good grief, where had I been all her life? I lingered in the shop trying out lipsticks, striping my wrist red and pink, letting what she'd said sink in: Blair might not wake up. The pharmacist started sweeping the shop and I didn't move. I continued trying out lipstick after lipstick until he flipped the CLOSED sign and rattled his keys.

The nurses are knocking off their shifts and squirting perfume on their wrists to get shot of the hospital stink. I pass them on the steps, buttoning jackets with fur collars over their uniforms and folding their hats into their bags like wee paper ships. There are a hundred places they could be flitting off to, up and away from all this sickness. I watch one lassie get on the back of a motorbike and wish I could join her. I can. I don't have to go in. I don't have to do nothing. Why should I? Blair. Blair with all her snidey comments on my clothes and a laugh like a demented horse whenever she sees me in that jumper Nan knitted with arms like King Kong.

I turn around and turn back. I'm picturing Lorrie's lip liner going all wonky. I let her slather make-up all over me, but it still didn't cheer her up. When she gripped an eye pencil she got this look on her face like a lassie with a colouring book concentrating on staying inside the lines, but it wore off fast. The sadness caught up with her.

'What if they're right and Blair never wakes up?' Lorrie held up a mirror.

I didn't know what to say. I still didn't when Ma came in later and saw me all dolled up. 'Look at the state of you,' she said. 'What do you think you look like?'

I thought: I look like a lassie doing something for her pal, but only a smidge of what she can.

There's a load of folks with balloons, flowers and bags of grapes in the hospital corridor. I suck a sour plum, check my flask of water and wander along. God, I want to leg it. None of this has anything to do with me. I could scarper and no one would be any the wiser. Then there's Lorrie . . . I keep walking along past the wards. There's a lady with a balloon visiting a toddler in a small room with an open door. I won't look. I can't. There's so much heartache I feel I'm breathing it in. It reeks. I can't stop it. I can't cheer everyone up. Not now. I just can't. I wish I could.

'Sylvie?'

I kinda know it's Joe before I even look up. I'd recognise his feet anywhere. The loops of his laces are perfectly even, like a wee lad who does everything carefully, fearty of getting it wrong.

'What you doing here?' he's saying.

'Nothing. Just visiting someone. What about you?'

Joe lifts his arm and lets it do all the talking. The cast is finally off. Underneath, his hand is so skinny and pale it doesn't look like it's his. It's the hand of a bairn.

'This useless thing.' He tries to make a fist and his fingers barely move. 'Nerve damage or something. I'm getting another opinion. They doubt I'll be able to play guitar any more, not the same way anyway.'

'I'm sorry,' I say.

I look down the corridor at Joe's ma punching a vending machine for a bar of Turkish Delight. I creep past her without looking up.

There's a bee hovering by the open window in Blair's room, deciding whether to come in or buzz off. I stare at it for ages instead of looking at her. The lass is peely wally. Her breathing's soft as an airbed going down. It's funny, she doesn't look mean when she's asleep. She just looks like a lassie who could do with a wee bit of sun. She doesn't look snidey or slutty or wild. She doesn't look that different to me. I put my fingers on her wrist and feel her pulse through my fingertips. I gulp and lower my head, so close a wisp of her hair wavers when I whisper in her ear.

'Blair, can you hear me? If you want to wake up, now would be a good time.' I wait for her to wake, pray for it. Beg. God, she doesn't move. I swallow, only vaguely aware of a face at the door as I lean in and kiss the girl.

LORRIE

There was no one to ask about the vandalism in the toilets. Sylvie was absent from school again. I called for her, but Bunny wouldn't allow her to come to the door. The closest I could get to Sylvie was hearing her name being whispered everywhere. Girls crammed into the toilet stall and stroked the word on the door they'd never dared say out loud. *Sylvie Johnson is a . . .*

'Now, enough dawdling. You'll be late for class.' Miss Stone checked the toilets for stragglers and marched us to gym, where the vaulting horse was already set up. Blair was back. She walked along the beam, every eye in the room on her.

'What was it like, being in a crash?' Marjorie Swift asked. 'When you were unconscious could you hear us? Did you know what was going on?' The class queued at the climbing wall, inspecting Blair for injuries. Her skin was flawless, her eyes were bright as a smashed windscreen.

'It was odd, it was like being locked out of the house and seeing what's going on inside through a foggy window,' Blair said. 'I couldn't find my keys and walk in. I could hear my mother sniffling though, and friends talking to me, but I couldn't sit up and join in. I couldn't move.'

I suspected Blair was making it all up, relishing the attention. She hadn't spoke to me since she left the hospital. Whatever friendship we'd had was as crumpled as the bumper on Dobby's car; it was easier to rip it off than beat it into shape. I was right about one thing, she insisted no one was drinking. Quite the opposite, Dobby was a gentleman. The pair had officially become an item. Blair told everyone they didn't fall in love, they crashed into it.

'You've got to hear this, you wouldn't believe what happened when I woke up.' Blair lowered her voice, a cluster of girls in PE skirts huddled in. I'd heard it before. The urge to gossip had been building up inside Blair while she was sleeping, and no one could stop it all bubbling out. 'I started to wake up and I felt something, someone's lips on mine. I opened my eyes and guess who I saw? Sylvie.'

My classmates turned towards me in the absence of Sylvie to stare at.

'You have to wonder, she's Lorrie's friend. Do you think they're . . .?'

Blair laughed. I knotted the laces of my plimsolls before walking over.

'What's your problem?' My fists curled at my sides.

'Nothing. I'm having fun with my girlfriends.' Blair laughed. 'You know how it is. You and Sylvie are girlfriends, aren't you? In a different way though.'

'Ladies . . .'

The teacher clapped her hands for us to move the gym mats into the alcove. Blair and I took one side of a mat apiece and sloughed it across the floor.

'Your little friend kissed me,' Blair said. 'She ran off as soon as I opened my eyes. But I saw her. She kissed me right on the lips.'

The mat slid onto the pile. Blair strolled away. I placed a hand on her shoulder, pulled her around and punched her face. I'd wanted to do that to someone all my life, to know how it felt. It was a let-down. The punch made no cowboy smack. The girl didn't land flat on the floor, her fingers stroked her cheekbone, more surprised than wounded. I was more damaged than her. Walking away, I uncurled my fingers and saw crescent moons, every fingernail snapped, clutched in my hand. I saw them all fall to the ground.

I stood under the shower letting the anger wash out of me. Blair was a liar. She loved being the centre of attention and would say anything to keep it that way. Sylvie would never visit her. And yet, I considered it. I had thought Sylvie was going to kiss me once. I'd burnt my hand making caramel, the skin had glowed and blistered, fire red. It was so painful I held my finger under the tap, wincing and hopping from foot to foot. 'You poor thing. It looks sore.' Sylvie came closer to inspect the wound, put her arm around me and stood so close her face was only inches from mine. There was an aroma of sour plums I could almost taste. She'd stared at my mouth and pulled away suddenly. 'It's just a burn,' she said. 'It hurts, but it will get better on its own.' I don't know why, but I thought about it later, alone in my room. I wondered what it would have been like to kiss her, she'd have done it softly, I thought. I'd have laughed afterwards and felt quiet for a long time.

I fumed in the changing rooms, forced to sweep sweet wrappers and dust out from under the benches for fighting.

'You can go,' Miss Stone said. 'I won't send a letter to your parents this time.'

I wandered through the school. The chairs were piled on the desks. The deserted corridors made my footsteps hollow. The building was quiet, other than for the sound coming from the music room. Joe Clark was sitting on a desk with his legs crossed, holding a guitar, one hand clawing the strings. He attempted to pluck, found he couldn't curl his fingers and shouted 'fuck'. I waited a second before going into the room.

'How's Sylvie?' he asked. 'Is she OK?'

'I don't know, haven't seen her. Bunny says she's got a stomach bug.'

'I hope she's alright. I saw her pass out last week. She didn't seem to know where she was.'

'At the hospital?'

'Yeah. I was in physio. My ma saw her fall. She had to phone her mother.'

'What day? When?'

'Thursday. I'm always there on Thursdays.' He held up his hand. 'Because of this stupid thing.'

The day Blair woke up, Sylvie was there.

I raced to Bunny's, wanting to ask Sylvie about Blair. I also wanted to tell her about punching someone, how it felt, and how I knew, now I'd done it, I'd probably do it again. It was a relief to let it all out. Bunny stepped onto the porch, closing the door behind her and blocking my view of a cardboard box in the hall.

'I need to talk to Sylvie. Can I pop up and see her?'

'She's too poorly for visitors,' said Bunny. 'She needs her rest.'

'Please, for a second, I have to see her.'

'Lorrie, you're sweating.' Bunny was the sort of person who usually said 'ladies perspire, horses sweat', but today she forgot this. 'I'll let her know you called,' she said, closing the door. I began to walk away and heard it open behind me. Bunny rushed after me. 'Oh, I forgot. I baked more than I need. Take some of these for your mother and Toby.' She handed me a box of biscuits shaped like rabbits with raisins for eyes.

I said 'thanks', omitting the 'for nothing'. I was always saddled with manners, even when I was fuming. Just as Bunny would always be the perfect neighbour, even when she wouldn't let you in.

The sun never really set that night. When I arrived on the island I could barely sleep during summer and my mother had to line my curtains with blackout fabric. Sylvie was never bothered by it, nor did she share my sense of injustice when it started to get dark at 3 p.m. in November. 'It all balances out, the sky's saving itself for June,' she would say. 'We get longer days than anyone then.'

I looked at Sylvie's window from mine, pointing a torch, unsure whether she could see it in the dusk. I switched the light off and on, using the same code we'd had when we were kids. One flash for, 'it's me, I'm here'. One flash back for, 'I know, so am I'. I'm here, I flashed, I'm here, I'm here, but nothing flickered back. Bunny strolled to the window, knotted her dressing gown and snapped the curtains closed without leaving a chink.

Everything swirls. The stairwell, the tiles under my feet, the double doors leading outside. The sky spins around the open mouths of strangers. Every ray of light swirls into one like a Van Gogh night full of stars. I don't know where I end and everything else begins. I don't know nothing, except Ma's shoving the strangers out of the way and kneeling on the grass.

'She's fine. Stand back. She needs air,' she says. 'I'm here now, don't worry, hen. I'll get you to your bed.'

I shut my eyes. Ma's dragging me up. I look down at her pointy shoes with the scuff on one toe. We're stepping all over the daisies. They're bleeding sap all over our shoes.

'Perhaps she's really poorly. The hospital's just there . . .'

The lady I saw with the balloon points to the building. Ma steers me clear of her to the car.

'There's no need. She's just a wee bit anaemic. You know how lassies are, always skipping lunch.'

I look out the window. The whole world's like an overexposed photograph, folks overlapping all over, a blur of stares and mouths. Mrs Clark's in the centre of the crowd, yattering to the woman who no longer has a balloon.

'That's outrageous . . .'

The woman's gasping and shaking her head. *Sheesh!* Mrs Clark's smirking and nodding.

'I'll just get her home,' Ma calls out the window. Teeth gritted into a smile. 'I appreciate you calling me, Mrs Clark, and letting me know you saw her.'

The car is screeching away with a salute of a wave. I press my face against the cold window. The clouds and grass are rushing at me so fast I get dizzy. Ma's smile snaps off like a lamp as soon as we're out of sight.

'What have you done now, Sylvie? What have I told you? For Christ's sake. That vile Mrs Clark saw what you were doing. She'll tell everyone. Damn it, Sylvie.' Ma blasts the horn at a post van outside a farm forcing us to stop at a passing place. 'Just wait until I get you home.'

She's storming, but I can't watch her change colours. My eyes keep wanting to close. I can't keep them open if I try. Even she knows that. The repercussions of my actions will have to wait until the world stops spinning. Ma keeps yelling anyway. She yells until we pull into the lane and we're staggering upstairs.

'This was so much easier when you were little, and it was only wounded robins and butterflies you kept finding everywhere. Christ, you're a dead weight.' She pants with the effort of lifting me into bed. 'A girl, of all things, Sylvie. What will people say? These things get around.'

Ma's nose goes all shiny when she's fuming and doesn't know how to let it out like a lady. She's a kettle bubbling on the inside with only the weeniest spout to let the steam out. I can't watch her boil. I can't move my gob and my head's pounding even when she puts a wet flannel on it.

When I wake up she's wearing her least favourite dress. It's laundry day, and she's had time to calm down, but she's not forgotten anything. She's pacing my room waiting for me to wake up. The arm on my wee record player's been snapped off and she's been rummaging through the shelves.

'I don't think it was wise for me to get you this . . . some wee lassie wandering off chasing rabbits, getting crazy ideas from grinning cats. I have a mind to go through all your books and see what else can go.'

I boak over the bed. Not the books. I'm gagging and gagging and nothing comes up. Ma brings a bucket and rubs my back, baby style.

'Honey, I'm home!' Seth calls the same greeting he's been using for years. He saw it in a movie somewhere.

'Put the kettle on, I'll be right down.' She fixes a smile on her face and hisses. 'This isn't over.'

Click. The door locks behind her on the way out. I can hear her singing while she cooks tatties. She's singing so no one would guess she's dying to shout.

LORRIE

There was more graffiti when Sylvie returned to class. It was scratched into her chair with a compass. It was a word no one spoke, though some mouthed it in slow syllables after the ladies who sold wool left the craft shop. The women kept llamas. No one on the island had ever seen one before. When the animals had arrived in a shipping container, a crowd gathered to see them spit and hiss at anyone who looked their way. People watched the women direct the crate to their field and stand by the fence admiring the strange creatures, leaning against one another and smiling. They'd had a plan to breed the animals, and they were successful. They really did produce the softest wool, though some refused to buy it. They disapproved of the women living together like that, without men. Sylvie liked them though. We used to go up there with apples in our pockets, stretching our hands over the fence to feel the llamas snuffle our palms. One time, the woman with the shorter hair saw us and waved, calling her friend out from her spinning wheel: 'Hey, Peggy, we've got visitors. Peggy.' She called again and started singing 'Peggy Sue' to the woman walking towards us. She laughed, 'Her name's Peggy Anne, but I still can't help singing it!' The woman had a strong voice, louder than the wind.

'Don't mind this lunatic,' Peggy said. 'Maggie will sing to anything! I hear her singing from dusk till dawn. It's not even just songs, she sings what she's doing! We'll make supper, and she'll make up a song about chopping onions. We'll milk the goat, and she'll sing a song about goats.'

'What's wrong with that? If you've got the voice, you may as well use it.' Maggie grinned.

Before we knew it, we were all singing, stroking the llamas. The women told us we could feed the llamas anytime, but we never went again. Bunny forbade it, even when Sylvie offered to drop off a kitchenware catalogue and potentially get a sale.

The staff spoke in assembly about the importance of valuing school property, without wanting to mention precisely what the graffiti said. They didn't need to, we all knew. Last Sunday in church, Bunny had been forced to sit at the back with the coughers. For as long as anyone could remember she had sat in the second row from the front, but no one scooched up for her. The women sitting there had spread their legs, put their bags on the pew and said, 'There's no room, Bunny, you'll have to sit somewhere else.' Bunny smiled, but everyone had been able to see she was blushing. She'd stood up straight and gone elsewhere, pretending not to hear The Island Mothers whispering what Mrs Clark had told them she'd seen Sylvie do. The women had one or two things to say about Bunny Johnson. 'And she sold me a duff biscuit barrel too, airtight my arse.'

I kept my distance from Sylvie in the corridor, not wanting to be dragged into the gossip about her.

'Did you visit Blair?' I asked.

'Course not.'

'Joe Clark said he saw you.'

'He probably saw someone who looks like me,' Sylvie mumbled.

I inspected the long dress and cardigan Bunny had made for her: shapeless and beige. It reminded me of saints who wore hessian as penance. Only Sylvie would ever wear something so drab. It didn't seem possible Joe could have mistaken her for anyone else, but I didn't get the opportunity to push it. Bunny was charging through the double doors at the end of the corridor, followed by a line of mothers carrying cardboard boxes. Bunny was a wonderful saleswoman. With baked goods and passionate speeches, she'd found a way to win them over since they snubbed her in church. The problem wasn't her daughter. Oh no, look around, the problem was the notions being put into young heads about sex. Their children had to be getting their ideas from somewhere. The women began a crusade.

'Good afternoon, girls.' Bunny and the women streamed into the library.

Sylvie ran after her. 'Why you here, Ma? What are you doing?'

'It's a small matter concerning suitable reading material. Don't worry, darling, it's none of your concern. The Island Mothers had a meeting about it. It's all been decided.'

The women shook their heads and placed books into boxes. Bonnie Campbell stood by the checkout desk, still clutching her library stamp. Her hands dangled at her side, unsure what to do, the library stamp leaving ink on her skirt.

'Ma, no! Please don't, I'll behave. I promise.' Sylvie gripped Bunny's arm.

The librarian placed a hand on Sylvie's shoulder, pulling her back, 'It's alright, Sylvie,' she said. 'I knew this was coming. The faculty approved it. No one wants the press involved. One of the women has a husband who works for the *Highland Herald*. The whole island will look like fools.'

Bonnie let Sylvie cry on her shoulder. The women streamed past with full arms.

Sylvie grabbed a book from one of their boxes. 'What's wrong with this, Ma? There's no harm in this one, surely? Please . . .'

One of the other women answered on Bunny's behalf. 'Witches, girls woken by a kiss, that dreadful girl in red shoes. It all starts somewhere, it pollutes the impressionable.'

'That's right.' Bunny accompanied the woman outside. Sylvie stroked the clean strip on the shelves where the books had once been.

'I'm sorry,' she said.

The librarian shushed her. 'It's OK. There won't be any scandal at least, since we allowed the books to be removed. It will blow over. Next month they'll have another bee in their bonnet and we'll be able to read whatever we want.'

Bonnie put her arm around Sylvie, but Sylvie wouldn't stop mumbling, 'It's all my fault.'

The fire sputtered to life, smoke pluming into the air. The women huddled in Bunny's garden waiting for baked potatoes and watching the books burn. The pages curled. The paper fumed into sepia and ash drifted into the air, quiet as snow. Bunny folded her arms, staring at Sylvie across the flames. Sylvie raced upstairs. She'd let the books burn without her. She couldn't look. I sat in her bedroom waiting for the fire to be over. The air smelt of charred paper even indoors.

'She's only doing it to punish me.'

Sylvie rubbed her eyes. Their colour changed with her mood, sometimes they looked blue. Other days, not so much. Today they were grey.

'Punish you for what?' I asked.

'Nothing.' Sylvie scratched her knuckles and sucked the wound.

'It's not like they were your books. The library can get more,' I said, but it was ash in the air. Whatever I said drifted over Sylvie's head, doing nothing to soothe whatever was going on in there.

'I can't do anything right. Even when I think I'm doing the right thing, it's wrong.'

The record player Seth had given her was broken. We could listen to nothing but the canary singing so loudly we barely heard the tap on the door. Seth stood outside holding out a plate of baked potatoes, a butter-filled offering for his stepdaughter who was sad for reasons he didn't understand. Everything was rosy in his marriage, so long as they never talked about religion and he never expressed an opinion on his wife's disciplining of the girl.

'You didn't have any supper, I thought you might be hungry,' he said.

Sylvie accepted the plate. It was as close as admitting he didn't agree with Bunny as Seth would get. We sat on the bed eating potatoes, butter glossing our lips. Sylvie stared past me to the spaces on her bookshelf. All she had left were flowers and birds.

'I can't stand it here,' she said. 'I've had it. Things are going to change from now on.'

I had no idea what she meant. I looked at her and thought her eyes looked less grey. They contained flecks of hazel bright as flames catching a page.

13TH JUNE 1960

Life goes on like normal, on and on. There are suppers to dollop, crusty bits of fish pie to scrape out of the pot, and pretty pastel sandwich boxes to sell. Everything looks perfect, but it's not. Ma's smile is rickety as a lid on a pressure cooker about to pop. So is mine. I seethe, polishing the fireplace, bringing the laundry down from my room. I'm cleaning everything so much the Virgin Mary looks bollock-naked, all the blues in her robes rubbed away.

Ma won't raise her voice when her husband's around. Neither do I. Zach glances at Seth for answers to the silence hanging between us. Seth shrugs. It's a women thing. Best not to ask.

'Oh look, a letter off your grandmother.' The ivory paper flaps in Ma's hand. 'We should visit one weekend soon, Sylvie. Won't that be fun?'

'I'm not going,' I say.

'Of course you are.' She pours pork crackling into a bowl and puts it on the occasional table for the boys. Everything's so light in their presence, so sweet and just as it should be. I could scream.

I'm not even going to read the letter. I reckon I know what it says. Nan's got arthritis, a cough, bunions on her toes, a cold she caught off that foul boy in the post office. So off we'll go to an island even smaller than ours. We'll take rat traps and jars of rowanberry jelly, and wild flowers that will be wilting before we even arrive. Ma will take a bag full of knitting to finish like she always does. She can cast on, knit and purl as well as anyone else, but she can never cast off without getting it wrong. Nan has to do it for her every single time. There are loads of women here on the island she could ask, but she won't. She's convinced they'll see she doesn't know everything and judge.

Seth never joins us when we go to Nan's and Ma never asks. It's a place where no one gets to eat unless they say their prayers. The cottage is all nooks and crannies filled with portraits of saints and psalms embroidered on tea towels. It's nowhere Seth wants to go, but, sometimes, I reckon it's not only that. Ma doesn't want him to come and see who she was before she was Bunny, just a lanky wee lassie with knees like sandpaper from dropping to her knees to say her prayers all day long. She couldn't wait to get out of there, stop being called Theresa and start calling herself by her favourite pet name.

'That swear box of yours must be full about now,' she's saying to Seth. 'The church could do with the gutters replacing. You're so busy, I suppose it's a trip for us girls again.'

'I think Seth and Zach should come,' I say.

Ma looks daggers at me. Only one person needs to come. And I know it. We clear out Ma's new fridge while the boys watch a movie about Spitfires and guns. I pick a pot of cream off the counter and hand her it to place on the shelf.

'I'm not going anywhere,' I whisper. 'I'm not doing you a favour again. Not that kind.'

The sound of an aeroplane is droning through the living room. Panic crosses Ma's face like she knows I mean what I'm saying. She wipes the cheese drawer and says, 'You have to come, it's your own flesh and blood.'

I have a bunch of fond memories of Nan buried in the back of my head somewhere. Sitting on her knee and being shown how to finger-knit. Her hand clutching mine, guiding a wooden spoon around a bowl, showing me the secrets of fruit cake. And it doesn't matter. I'm done. There's no memory strong enough to wipe out the stink of the burnt books and the sight of Ma in the library in front of everyone. I'm done. I'm done. I'm done. I think it like the chorus of a song, closing the fridge. I watch for the light going out.

LORRIE

There was a moment my mother forgot everything, when she was serving dinner. I saw her bring out a plate for my father, place it on the table, blink, and put it back on the shelf without saying anything. Other than that, we forgot nothing. We cringed at the slightest sound, all prepared for the same thing: a police officer knocking on the door, removing his hat, holding the battered briefcase my father always carried his lunch in, sopping wet and covered in sand.

The phone rang as the distillery closed for the day. My mother picked it up with her keychain in her hand. I pressed my ear to the other side of the receiver. We gathered around it holding our breath.

'You might want to come over. I've got your husband here . . . No. No, he's not injured, not that I can see anyway. I found him outside, feeding the ducks,' a man said.

I sensed something restraining him from telling the whole story. He sounded ashamed.

'That was Mr Fletcher. Your father's fine.' My mother set down the phone.

'Where's he been? Where did he go? Why?' Toby asked.

'I don't know the details. He's on the mainland, on our old street. Safe. That's all that's important. We can bring him home.'

She left the room to collude with Grumps in the hall. Someone had to drive out and collect my father, casually as a parcel. It didn't occur to any of us he'd return to England. He'd been so willing to leave it. It was rare to hear him speak about the life we'd left behind. None of us really did any more. Whenever I thought of it, I found more and more of the details had disappeared. I visualised my old bedroom and saw only the wardrobe in my current room, the yellow paint on the walls. There was too much living going on to cling to the life that was gone.

If my father still had any friends in the city, he didn't so much as send them a Christmas card. Grumps pumped up his tyres for the journey and Mum called the baker for more information.

'He's OK? Can I speak to him? Will you put him on?'

'You should really get down here. I don't want to talk on the phone.'

Grumps finally pulled up with insects splattered on the windscreen and my father slumped in the back seat asleep. The journey had taken almost two days. It was barely morning.

'Here he is,' Grumps whispered. 'Longest drive of my life. He sat in the back like a lady with a chauffeur, didn't mutter a word the whole way.'

My father stood in the kitchen in his socks, looking around, a visitor in his own house. There was no sign of his jacket. He wore only a grubby shirt, splashed with gravy.

'Where have you been? The kids were worried. You could have let us know.'

My mother hugged the relief out of herself and pulled away from him. The look on her face reminded me of when Toby or I used to wander off at the zoo; she'd hug us for a second and then scold us for so long we wondered why we hadn't stayed away. Grumps waved her to come to the hall to speak about something he didn't want to be overheard.

'He was hanging around the bakery. The baker said he gave him this.'

Grumps produced a cheque from his breast pocket.

'That's our savings. It's pretty much everything we have.'

My mother inspected the cheque and glanced towards the door, unsure who the man on the other side was.

'It was decent of the fella not to cash it. When I arrived, he had no shoes on his feet, Cora. There was no sign of the car.'

She looked at her husband sitting in the same place as always, cutting a slice of bread at the table and buttering it to the edges.

'You're back!' Toby raced downstairs in his pyjamas, and stalled. He couldn't quite hug his father. None of us could. Our arms had dangled at our sides our whole lives, strained by tense situations, unsure how to dive into deep waters we weren't prepared for. Ours was a family who cared at a distance. My mother served food and swept up the crumbs. Grumps opened whisky and offered a glass. How my brother and I showed how we felt was less clear. We hadn't figured it out yet.

'Everything's OK, son, I'm fine.'

Dad sliced more bread. Toby sat opposite him, matching him chew for chew. I remained by the pantry, eavesdropping on the conversation in the hall.

'Where's the car?' My mother stroked her collarbone.

'I don't know,' Grumps said. 'The baker saw him give the keys to some homeless fella and point to it across the street. Keep an eye on him, Cora, if you're not careful he'll give your whole life away. What was he thinking?'

'I have no idea. I only live with him.' My mother returned to the kitchen to boil milk and honey. 'You're alive, anyway, that's all that matters,' she repeated.

'Where's your shoes?' Toby asked. Someone had to. We

glanced at my father's socks under the table – holes in the heel, an oval of black on the sole.

'Oh, that.' He looked down at his feet. 'I gave them away.'

'Who to? Why?'

'Someone who needed them more than I do. I never caught his name. Nice fella. He was looking for a job.'

Grumps poured a whisky, shaking his head. My mother accepted a glass, took out a jar of marmalade and placed it on the breadboard. My father ate and ate. He ate for so long we wondered if he'd ever stop. We looked at him waiting for his mouth not to be full, wanting him to explain. He didn't offer another word.

'Now, Toby, Lorrie, time to get dressed. We have to get back to normal around here.' My mother looked at my father, wondering if we'd ever get there. She had no idea if the journey would take days, weeks, or years.

I know where to find him. I'm dead sure. I reckon some folk never change. Their habits run right through them like knots in wood. They can get dead tall, grow sideys and a fuzzy wee moustache, but really they're just the same.

I find him on his own in that spot near where he lives. He's nestled into that crack in the oak tree a fork of lightning made into the perfect seat. Clutching his guitar. The fingers on his busted hand are wrapped around its neck, struggling with a chord.

'Do you want to play that thing? Seriously?' I say. 'Why?'

Joe looks so surprised to see me I start laughing. I'm always surprising to him.

'It's the only thing that makes me feel like someone else,' he says. 'Someone better.' He's lowering his head and his hair's going all floppy over his eyes 'I wish something else made me feel that way, anything. When I'm not playing I'm nothing. Or I feel it, anyway.'

I look at him and it's crazy. I can sorta see a boy on the sidelines, watching folk race by. He drags that kid he used to be about everywhere. Other than when he's making music, he's always there.

'You happy when you play?' I say.

'As happy as I know how to be.'

'Close your eyes' – I take a step towards him – 'and put down the guitar.'

'What . . .? Why?'

'Trust me. Stand up. Just close 'em.'

Joe closes his eyes and his eyelids flicker like candles at Christmas. He's twitchier than a wee lad waiting for Santa, faking sleep, listening to his stocking being filled with oranges and tin cars. I put my palm on his chest and think of a sparrow that once flitted into the kitchen, flapping for a window. I kiss him and see broken wings. I raise my hands to his shoulders. And cling. The flick of his tongue in my mouth stops in a heartbeat. I'm staggering all over. Fingers curled, I'm grabbing his shirt so tight a button flies. It's a struggle to keep standing up.

'Sylvie? Are you OK?' Joe holds me by my shoulders. I'm floppy as soggy washing on a line.

'I'll be fine in a wee bit. I just have to sit for a minute.'

'You sure you're alright?' He gets on his knees to meet my eye. I sit and he sits beside me, stroking his lips like the kiss I gave him was Braille.

'How's that hand of yours?' I say. Mine's aching as if I punched a flipping wall. Joe curls his fingers.

'Better. Wow, so much better.' He's wriggling his fingers, straightening 'em up, wriggling them some more. He's trying them out like something new. They dance over the strings of his guitar. I close my eyes, jolt awake. I can't fall asleep here.

'Wow.' Joe keeps moving his fingers. 'I feel like I could throw a ball to the moon.'

I smile with my back to the oak. Joe leans in to kiss me. Just kiss me. Not because he's wounded, just because. I turn my head.

'You won't kiss me again, will you?' he says. 'Ever?'

'I don't think I can kiss anyone,' I say. 'Not for fun anyway.'

Our knees are barely touching as we sit on the ground, side by side.

'If you could, though, would you?' he says.

We look at each other, knowing things we won't say.

'If I could kiss anyone, Joe Clark, it would be you.'

'And I'd let you, Sylvie Johnson,' he says.

Neither of us move. For ages and ages, we sit side by side, one knee against another saying hello and goodbye. We won't kiss again. And we know it. We'll barely speak. This, sitting here, knee to knee, is the closest to an admission of something we'll ever get. We're letting go of it at the same time. Joe Clark kinda likes me. I kinda like him. And it's over before it even begins.

The dead owl thumped into the bin. Grumps clanked on the lid, shaking his head.

'I can't look at an owl without thinking of my cousin. We weren't supposed to knock about together. Our fathers hated each other, but we'd meet up sometimes in the woods. That kid's wild bird calls sounded so convincing he could call the owls out of the trees. He was a decent kid before he was a crazy old man.'

My mother wasn't listening. Everything had to get back to normal around here. There were no hotels on her husband's bank statements. No flowers, or fish suppers, and that meant no woman. He'd slept in his car until the car was gone (that's the word he used, 'gone', as if giving it away had been out of his hands). Seth Johnson knew someone who could get him a deal on a Ford identical to the one he'd given away. He could put on the same jacket and return to work the same as always.

Mum placed rock cakes on a chopping board after dinner. The kitchen filled with the aroma. We discussed the dessert, none of us knowing what else to say.

'One of your favourites.' She set about salvaging the buns, scraping a burnt strip from one of the edges. She'd never be a great cook, but she served her failures as treats. We pretended they were.

Dad picked up a currant and chewed. He didn't say much, but then he never had. It was a different sort of silence to the one we were used to. Sylvie was right. Once, when Bunny was annoyed with her, she told me there are a hundred different sorts of silence. Sometimes when she wasn't speaking she was fine, and just looking at things, and sometimes she wasn't. Sylvie said silence has more shades than there are colours on a chart. I listened to the sounds she was making at the time, but not the words. I only understood after my father went missing. There were so many different silences in the house I couldn't bear it.

One silence belonged to my father, looking beyond us as we sat around the table. He stood and, without saying a word, carried a fistful of rock cake outside. We stayed where we were sitting, aware of him ripping it into pieces for the birds.

The silence of my mother was the sound of water. She got up and washed the dishes slowly, wondering what separated her husband from us all.

Then there was my grandfather's silence. His was a container holding everything he could only let out once his son-in-law had left the room.

'Now a woman would make sense,' he said. 'If he'd left for some floozy. Or even drink, but this . . .'

He understood those men who grabbed whatever they could to lose a part of themselves. Men like that lived in the country and the city alike – the only thing that changed was the sheen of their shoes and the roughness of their hands grabbing a glass. Ambition was a dangerous thing. The one thing every broken man he'd ever met had in common was they'd all wanted more than they had, and felt they should have amounted to more.

'He needed a holiday, that's all.' My mother scraped the scorched baking tray. 'Who doesn't want to disappear sometimes? He's fine now.'

The sparrows hopped close to my father outside, pecked a crumb, and hopped back. The word in the village shop was the man was crazy, she knew that. Crazy, not in a raving sort of way, but the quiet sort of crazy you can't trust. There could be no other reason a man would give up his vehicle.

I saw her defend him as much as she could, but it didn't convince anyone.

'Why is it crazy for him to want to give someone something?' she said. 'Bunny Johnson's constantly donating to the church, Seth too, and the church gives to the poor. No one calls that crazy.'

Grumps didn't reply. Over the years, he'd often wished his son-in-law would vanish. When it finally happened, it was another thing he couldn't get right. He could have gone wild with drink, screamed at his wife, or run off with a girl half his age. It would have been better than this. His daughter would scream, kick him out and get it over and done with. This wasn't so simple. The man was still here, though only his body. His thoughts were elsewhere. We all noticed but we went along with it. There didn't seem to be any other option than pretending nothing had changed.

Ma's perching on the balls of her feet like she's searching for someone lost in a crowd. That tiny hat she loves is pinned to her head. The ivory suitcase waits in the hall with her gloves all folded up and lying on the clasp. We're supposed to be off, setting out to my nan's as soon as I get in. And here I am, dead late. Wobblier than Bambi on my feet, Joe's arm around my waist. With baby steps, we walk up the path.

I whisper, 'I'll be fine from here.' I pull away and sag.

'I've got you.' His arm stays around me. Firm. I can smell the washing powder on his shirt. And soap, and that boy smell I sorta wish they sold in a bottle so I could dab it on my pillow and breathe it in.

'Where do you think you've been, missy? What's this?' Ma's dragging me off Joe.

'She came over faint, Mrs Johnson. I wanted to make sure she got home alright,' Joe says.

I wonder how such a soft voice doesn't get lost in the size of him, just get swallowed up.

'You! I know what you've been doing. I know all about it. Believe me, mister.' Ma turns to me. 'And now you're too poorly to visit your nan. Are you satisfied?'

I am. Ma pulls me inside, unbuckles my shoes and leaves them on the mat.

'What have I told you about that boy? He used you,' she says.

'No, he didn't.' I say. I'm smiling even though I'm giddy. I reckon I used him to feel good about myself.

I crawl under the blankets and bury myself, dormouse style. Joe's happy. He can play his guitar again just like he's supposed to. And Ma can do nowt about it. She's drawing the curtains and saying something about being grounded until I'm twenty-one. I don't care. I close my eyes and drift off to a land where girls kiss boys who feel they could throw a ball all the way to the moon. Ma can nag for a month of Sundays. And it won't change a thing. For once, she didn't get her way. Today, we won't be going to Nan's or anywhere else. I win.

LORRIE

Bunny's knock on the door was as crisp as her outfit. My mother let her in with a sigh.

The Singer stood on the dining table surrounded by cut fabric – a breast here, a collar there. It was difficult to imagine they could ever be made into anything that could dance.

'That dance is coming up. And we haven't even discussed it, we've been so busy,' Mum said, taking pains not to add 'with waiting for your father to be found'.

'I don't know if I want to go,' I said.

Blair was done with me. Sylvie was off school again and Bunny wouldn't let me in to see her. The dance was a lonely place, but I was going, my mother was adamant. I was starting to think sometimes there are dances daughters go to in frilly dresses simply to prove life is rosy.

Bunny picked up an offcut of satin, fingernails clicking on the pins. 'I bet there's not a kitchen for miles that doesn't resemble a dress factory right now. So many pins and spools of cotton everywhere. There's a solution, you know. I have the perfect item . . .' She opened the sturdy box she was carrying under her arm and placed a pin inside it. 'See! There are compartments for anything: cotton, needles, pins . . .'

'The cushion I keep the pins in works fine,' my mother said. She looked tired. Pretending everything was perfect had become a full-time job that was harder than it looked.

'You know, the church is having a pie and pea fundraiser. It would be lovely if you could help. We could always use another hand,' Bunny said.

'I don't have time.'

'You know, people say that. It's so sad. There's never time to help others. Everyone's so busy, busy, busy! Yet if everybody did a little, how different everything would be.' Bunny picked up a spool of cotton and reeled in the loose end. 'They get all over don't they? So difficult to store, always rolling off somewhere.'

My mother pulled her chequebook out of the sideboard. Whether it was buying the Greatest Sewing Caddy in the World, or dolloping mushy peas out at bingo night in the village, she had to give the woman something. It took so much energy to say no.

'Can Sylvie come to the dance?' I asked. 'Will she be better soon?'

'I doubt it,' Bunny said. 'You know Sylvie. Dances aren't her style. Besides, she's still ill.' There was a magazine on the sideboard. Bunny picked it up, flicked through and closed it. Now that she had a fridge, there was no need to clip contests to win one out of every magazine she saw lying around.

Mum looked up, pen perched on the cheque. I knew we both wanted to say the same thing – that perhaps Sylvie would be the sort of person who enjoyed dances, if Bunny let her be and gave it a chance.

'What's wrong with her, exactly?' she asked.

'Nothing to be concerned about. Sylvie suffers from allergies.'

'I thought you said she had chickenpox?'

Bunny folded the cheque and made the crease crisp with her fingernails.

'How is your husband, anyway? Did he enjoy his little holiday? It's funny he didn't tell anyone he was going anywhere . . .'

'He's right as rain. It's all my fault. He told me he was planning to visit friends months ago, I forgot to write it down,' my mother said.

The women's smiles were a wall. Bunny refused to reveal what was going on with Sylvie, and my mother refused to fuel gossip about my father. The truth was, none of us knew why he'd left, or whether he'd have come back on his own if he hadn't been found. It took all our energy not to ask. He was well in the sense that he got up, went to work, and came home on time. It would do. We no longer felt we knew him, but, thinking about it, we weren't sure we ever had.

It was foggy in the morning. We woke to find another owl on the step. My father saw it before anyone else. This one was small, a barn owl with a hundred eyes on its back. He put down his keys, cradled the bird and stared at it for a long time before striding across the lawn.

He took a spade from the shed and started to dig. When the hole was finished, he dropped to his knees and buried the owl, scooping the soil with his hands. There was a shudder to his shoulders, but I didn't go out to him. I'd never seen a man cry. I wouldn't know what to do. I didn't think I should see it. I didn't want my father to be human, I wanted him to be strong. I wanted him to be identical to the men I saw in the movies.

Once the owl had a grave, he brushed the dirt off his hands and left for work, the same as always. Mum came downstairs smelling of toothpaste, followed by Toby, bed hair sticking up everywhere. I didn't report what I saw. I pretended it hadn't happened. I looked above the patch of dirt where my father had been digging, determined not to look down until the grass grew again.

There's a whiff of cucumber when I open my eyes. Ma's sitting there like a salad, a minty looking face mask slapped all over, slices of cucumber laid on her eyelids. It's something she started doing in my bedroom as soon she got married, as if her beauty regime was some sort of deadly secret no man should see in case it killed him on sight.

'You're awake,' she says, and then *wham!* She dives into laying down the law.

'No cosmetics. No boys. No school. No sneaking through the fence to see Lorrie. I want you where I can see you, missy.'

Shite. She hasn't calmed down while I was sleeping. She's had the chance to plan my whole life.

'I don't want you going anywhere near Joe Clark. I've written to your Nan. You can go and stay with her until the whole Blair debacle blows over and tongues stop wagging.'

'I don't want to go,' I say. 'I was thinking of applying for a job at the launderette in the village when school's finished.' I reckon I'd be good at that. I love the shush of the machines and seeing all the clothes chasing each other around. I'd die before I let a purple sock slip in with the whites.

'You'll do what I say. The damage is done, Sylvie. People talk. Everyone has long memories here.'

It's true. Rumours linger in the village longer than the sound of the ocean stays inside a shell. If I'm not here to remind anyone, Ma hopes folk will stop yacking about what kinda lassie they think I am.

'It won't change anything,' I say. 'Wherever I go, I'll still be me.'

Ma peels off bits of face mask like a zombie with sunburn. She doesn't get it. The problem isn't one pal being a bad influence. Or one girl. Or one boy. It's not TV. Or rock and roll. Or books. It's being young. And being me.

'I only want what's best for you.' She gets up to scrub off the face mask before Seth sees. 'Tea will be ready soon. It's your favourite for pudding. Raspberry ripple.' She waits for me to say something to make her feel I realise she's on my side, in a suffocating sorta way.

'I'm not hungry,' I say.

'Have it your way.'

Ma closes the door. It won't stay closed forever. I could get out of my bed soon and walk through it. I could go to the village and get a job doing laundry. Or learn shorthand, and wear glasses, and get a wiggle skirt and hop over to the mainland to turn into a secretary. I could do whatever I want, as soon as I know what it is, anyway.

LORRIE

There was a smashed window at the distillery. The clouds looked into the glass on the ground, so did our faces and hands picking up the broken pieces. Grumps circled a patch of charred grass and entered the building to assess the damage. Several smashed bottles littered the slate floor, whisky pooled by the door. At his feet lay a dropped strip of damp matches.

'Could have been worse.' He picked up the matches. 'I think someone just wants me to know they could have burnt the place to the ground if they'd wanted to.'

The police officer scribbled on a notepad too small for his hands. He wanted to know who would do this. 'Perhaps you've had a falling-out with someone? Do you have any enemies?'

'No more than anyone.' Grumps showed the officer out. The cellar door remained locked. The barrels untouched. There were footsteps on the grass outside the shed where the finest malts were kept. Someone had stopped at the door and turned back, changing their mind, not bearing to go in.

Grumps breathed in the spilled liquid: 'Notes of syrup and spice. A decent batch.'

'We can claim for the window on the insurance,' my mother said, mopping up whisky. She looked around for my father to reassure her on the claim, but he'd already left us. Insurance was no longer his favourite subject. He was outside stroking the blackened grass, slipping off his shoes and socks and wiggling his toes in the unspoilt grass to recall how it felt. Mum turned to Rook, pouring her bucket of whisky suds down the drain.

'There's a lot to do around here. Rook, you'd better get on the phone and find a glazier.'

'I already did, Lucky,' he said. 'We'll have someone here before the day's out.'

Grumps shovelled glass into a sack. I held it open for him. We worked together outside in the late afternoon. Him shovelling, me clutching the hessian, bending to pick up shards. I didn't see the bearded man until Grumps did. He was standing across the lane, eyes narrowed, watching us work.

'I'll be damned . . .' Grumps chased after him faster than I knew an old man could move. He ran with the shovel still in his hand, dropping it halfway down the lane.

'Where you going? You shouldn't run. You'll have a cardiac!'

I ran after him, half limping, half running towards Abel West hobbling away. I slowed my pace before I caught up, eager to avoid meeting him again, wanting no one to realise we'd already met.

Grumps grabbed Abel's shirt and dragged him around to face him. There was a sound of ripping cotton as he shoved him against the hedge, a flurry of sparrows taking to the air. Grumps pushed Abel. Abel pushed back. The pair scuffled, rolling in the dirt lane. Without warning, they broke free in agreement, both placing a hand on their chests, catching their breath.

'It was you who tried to burn the place down,' Grumps said. 'I knew it.'

Abel grinned and flashed a colour chart of teeth, a progression of yellows and browns.

'What do you want?' Grumps asked. 'Lurking about the place with your owls. Well, spit it out. You've got my attention now. Now's your chance . . .'

Abel straightened his shirt and brushed down the ruffled fabric. He'd been sure his cousin owed him something all his life. Now he was being asked what he wanted, he was unsure what it was. He hadn't planned on getting the opportunity to present his opinion. No one ever asked him anything. In his derelict cottage, all winter he would imagine his cousin in a large house surrounded by women. He would picture a distillery full of bottles the colour of gold, and money piled high under a bed filled with feathers. The person facing him was an old man just like him, alone, charcoal on his fingers and smashed glass crushed into his soles.

'We knew whisky too,' he said. His voice was filled with spit. 'I coulda done good as you, if I'd got the chance.' Abel wiped spit off his beard. What he wanted sounded so foolish he felt small.

'I don't deny it.' Grumps picked grit out of his palm. 'Our old men both knew a thing or two. But what could mine do? Just hand over half a business his father worked all his life for? Would your da come to work for us for a decent wage? Course not. He was stubborn. We're all stubborn. Life isn't fair. I admit it.' Grumps shrugged. 'That what you wanted to hear? Will you leave me alone now?'

'Dunno,' Abel grunted. 'Got used to pissing on your door-knobs. Looked forward to it.'

Grumps nodded. If someone had seen them at a distance, the pair would have resembled two men discussing a hobby. They agreed being angry was as good a hobby as any.

'I get it, some things just get to be habit.' Grumps wiped his hand on his trousers, the hand that opened his door every morning. The men leant on a fence. One nodded. One shrugged. One offered his hand to be shaken. The other almost shook it, then waved it away. One lit the cigarette of the other and they shuffled off their separate ways. They might have smiled – no one could tell beneath their beards.

I wasn't sure precisely what changed. Nothing seemed to be have been achieved by the exchange. Birds still died, and, occasionally, one turned up on our door loosely wrapped in burlap. Whenever it happened on his birthday, Grumps would pick the bird up, look into the distance and grin, knowing there was an old man out there somewhere, still cursing, muttering, and thinking of him.

I'm just standing there at the kitchen counter munching cereal and gawping out at the garden. Ma's watching her shows in the living room. The canned laughter's bouncing off the walls. I don't go in and join her. The company of the sunset is enough. It moves across the land and paints everything rosy. I'm just watching it make the distillery peachy. Lorrie's da's popping into his potting shed. I see him come out carrying a gun.

It's funny, I've never seen him shoot anything before. Not for sport. Or to take pot shots at the dirty rats trying to nibble their way into the grain store. He props his father-in-law's gun on the bird bath and takes off his wedding ring. I see him pull his keys out of his pocket and lay them down in the dip where the birds wet their wings. Then he picks up the gun and wanders off to the distillery, leaving all his stuff behind.

I follow him out. Heart pounding. Cheeks burning. Knowing something's wrong.

He holds the gun steady, studies it for a while and presses it under his chin.

No. No. I want to yell, but the words are all jumbled. I open my mouth to call him and freeze. What's his name? I reckon I've never heard anyone say it. He's just Lorrie's dad.

You don't want to do that, I'm wanting to say. Except he does. I can see it all over him. I feel it when I get close to him. There are no broken bones here. Not in his hand gripping the gun, or in his neck I'm putting my arm around. Whatever's broken is buried. I stare at his long face, the frown lines like sad wee brackets around his mouth. I'm drowning when I kiss him. I'm all floppy and heavy. There's this pain in my chest like someone put a stone there I have to carry around.

The gun is falling to the ground. I keep my arms around him for ages and ages even though I don't want to. I'm so sad suddenly, so completely I can't move. It's funny. Everything feels pointless, but I don't want to cry. I've got this feeling that doesn't know a way out. The sadness moves through me like an old woman tiptoeing around the house, peering into each room and turning out the lamps.

Lorrie's father pulls away and looks at the gun in surprise.

'I don't know what I was thinking,' he says. 'I lost myself somewhere.'

I know. I don't feel the same as when I kissed a lad with a broken hand and my knuckles ached. Or when I put a tatty-winged red admiral in my mouth one November and couldn't move my arms for an hour. Instead, I've got all these thoughts buzzing around, chasing each other round and round my head. I'm failing at life. I disappoint everyone I know. If I wasn't here, I reckon it would be better for everyone.

Lorrie's father is walking into the distillery and putting the gun back in the cabinet where it belongs. And I don't even follow him to check he's OK. I stand outside. Drained. One hand on the wall propping me, stopping me from falling –

falling so hard
I'll never get up.

LORRIE

The day before the dance I finally got to see Sylvie. Bunny had been keeping me at bay. The lamp had flashed in Sylvie's window that week. I wasn't sure how long she'd been trying to reach me, but I saw it at midnight. I flashed my lamp back, wishing we'd come up with a more sophisticated system so we could say something more than 'I am here, so are you.'

Grumps and Rook shared a beer in the kitchen, discussing plans to increase production at the distillery. Mum reached across Rook and touched his hand, pointing to a plan of the building.

'You know, if we move this door to the other side it would be simpler for deliveries.'

Rook agreed. 'You're right, Lucky.'

'Aren't I always?'

They never needed a reason to laugh. It happened all on its own. Just outside the room, my father put on his shoes and slipped out for one of his strolls.

I snuck upstairs to try on my dress for the dance. I was going with my brother for no reason but my mother, who was looking forward to taking a photo and putting it in a frame. The dress rustled, a stiff net underlay beneath the red skirt. I wandered around the house, getting used to it, listening to the new sound of every move I made.

Sylvie raced outside in her nightdress. I saw her from the back room we only used at Christmas and for storing winter supplies. In bare feet, she bolted out of the gate and along to the distillery, forgetting to shut her back door. I followed her, wondering where she was rushing off to that was so important she'd forgotten her shoes.

I saw the pair from a distance and paused at the sight. Sylvie was kissing my father. I stared at the back of his cardigan, his hands dangling loosely by his side. He stood still for a while, shook his head, picked something up and went into the distillery. I ran at her, my dress rustling.

'What are you doing?'

Sylvie turned in her cotton nightgown, face blank as one of the dolls we used to cut out of paper, a row of pale girls holding hands. I let my fist fly, still thinking of those flimsy dolls, the hours we'd spent together doing childish things.

'What did you do?' I raised my arm to hit her again, but she was already down.

'I had to do it.' Sylvie made no attempt to stand up and fight me. She stayed on the ground, the hurt look on her face doing all her punching back for her.

'I can imagine.'

'He needed me,' she said. 'You don't understand.'

I could barely hear her over my own breathing. I could have killed her. I might have, if no one had stopped me.

'What's going on?' Bunny arrived, pointing her finger. 'What did you do to her? It's always the same with people. Leave her alone.' Bunny poked me and waved a slow hand in front of Sylvie, still on the ground. 'You OK, petal? How bad is it this time?' She held out a hand and, for a second, I could imagine the years they were alone. Just a mother and a shy child collecting eggs.

'They were kissing. Him. Her . . .' I pointed at Sylvie, unsure who to scream at. Sylvie, my father, or Bunny. I loathed them all.

Bunny glared at my father coming out of the distillery.

'You! Don't so much as look at my daughter again. I don't care what's wrong with you. Never again.' She turned to me. 'And you, Lorrie, you should be ashamed.'

She put an arm around Sylvie and guided her, staggering, punch drunk. I didn't realise I'd hit her so hard. I stared at the pair, unsure how everything had switched around somehow. Bunny had made it sound as if I was in the wrong.

'What have I told you, you can't solve everyone else's problems. You have to put yourself first,' Bunny whispered to Sylvie, steering her feet clear of thistles on the path.

'I'm not sure what happened,' my father said. I folded my arms to stop my hands shaking and turned my back on him, refusing to listen to a word he had to say. I wasn't sure if I would ever again.

I stay dead still while Ma's tucking me into my bed. I keep picturing the anger plastered all over Lorrie's face like a bit in a movie that gets stuck in your head. God, she was raging. I don't even blame her. I can't argue with it. I've no fight left in me. It would be better for everyone if I wasn't here.

'You shouldn't have done that. He's a married man – what will folk say?'

'I know,' I say. 'I'm sorry,' I say. I'm sorry I disappoint her. I'm sorry I upset Lorrie, but I'm not sorry I kissed him. He had the sort of sadness that was ice in his bones. It felt like all he could do was throw a coat over it, knowing it would never warm his insides. I'm sorry I had to do it, but there was nowt else I could do. Lorrie's disgusted. Ma's ashamed. And I can't do nothing to change it. I can only change where I am.

I lie awake after she goes. I keep starting to drop off and jolt upright, all these sad thoughts spinning around my head.

The day ahead is a pink streak when I sneak out of bed. I button my dress and walk downstairs with a wee suitcase and the jar of pennies Ma gives me for mucking out the chickens. I take all the money out of her purse and leave her bonnie blue handbag gaping open with the penny jar in its place.

I shouldn't be here. I can't be who everyone wants me to be. I can't change either. I don't even know if I want to. Or how.

My wristwatch says it's almost 5 a.m. It's getting lighter by the minute. The dew on the shaggy grass is a silver pelt. I stare at it like someone taking a photo of it. I wander to the gate and stop, looking up at Lorrie's window. The curtains are closed. Everyone's in their beds. I wander along the lane carrying my case in one hand. With the other, I flag down the van that delivers fresh bread.

'You're up and about early, going somewhere nice? You want a ride?' The delivery lad grins. I hop in.

LORRIE

Bunny carried the canary out in a plastic box, perched her foot on a spade and sliced into the stony ground. Sylvie had been gone for a week. The last time anyone saw her she was boarding the 6 a.m. ferry. 'She'll come back,' Seth had said. 'Don't you worry, Bunny.' He believed Sylvie would return, but he went around the island with Zach, sticking posters to lamp posts, asking anyone with any information to get in touch. No one did. The girl had disappeared.

I hadn't seen Bunny since the morning she knocked on our door.

'Have you seen Sylvie?' she'd asked. 'She wasn't in her bed this morning.'

'She probably went for a walk or something. Did she say anything to you about going somewhere, Lorrie?' My mother stood at the door looking at me, searching for answers.

'I haven't seen her.' I had refused to say more. I couldn't do that to my mother. She was oblivious to what had happened with Sylvie and my father. He had been in such a good mood that morning. Studying her grilling toast, he had told her she looked lovely, though she hadn't washed her face or done her hair yet.

'I love it wild,' he'd said. 'You look good. I don't tell you enough.'

If I didn't know better, I'd have sworn this wasn't my father.

This was a different man: relaxed, appreciative, interested in life. He didn't wander away or get irritated with Toby. He guessed which cup the balls were under and laughed when he got it wrong. Looking at him, I couldn't believe he'd touched Sylvie. It had to be her fault. I blamed her without really believing it. It was simpler than finding fault closer to home.

Bunny now placed a stone on the spot where she buried the canary. It was unusually quiet. There was a hush in the hedgerow as if every bird in the garden was paying its respects.

'He couldn't live without her.' Bunny picked the rabbit out of the hutch and held it to her chest. 'I don't blame you for being mad at Sylvie, Lorrie. I get that way myself often enough. She's special. People take advantage of her. You don't have to understand. I don't understand it myself.'

'I'm sure she's fine,' I said. 'Wherever she is. Not that I care.'

I wanted to slate Sylvie for not being as shy as she made out, but I couldn't. Bunny gazed at the rabbit and held it so tight she looked afraid to let go.

'Have it your way, Lorrie, be as angry as you want, but Sylvie's your friend. You might not like everything she does, but she is.'

She carried the rabbit to the house, leaving me on the other side of the fence. Sylvie wasn't special, and she wasn't my friend. If that was friendship, I didn't need it.

The ferry honks of spilled coffee and the sweeties some old lady's offering all the other passengers. I accept a lemon drop, pop it in my mouth and plonk myself near the window with a notepad on my knee.

Dear Ma,

I'm on a ferry, so my writing might look wobbly as the cursive we practised when I was six. It feels dead funny to write this. Other than wee notes in the kitchen or funny wee cards I made for Mother's Day, I don't think I've ever written to you before. I've never said anything I know you won't have something to say about. I won't be including a return address because I don't have one. And I know you'd show up and drag me back. I don't want anyone to come looking. This isn't about you, it's me.

I'm not as sad as I was just after I kissed Lorrie's father. It all started to fade as soon as I packed my suitcase. I'm not sad and I'm not angry. I was angry when you burnt the books, but I'm not any more. What I am is excited. I can write this without wondering if you'll walk in and disapprove. This feels like the first time I can think whatever I fancy without anyone looking over my shoulder. Don't worry, Ma, please. Plenty of folks leave a place and start over all the time. I might be different to them in some ways, but I'm also the same. I'm just another person, regardless of stuff I can and can't do. Who this person is, I don't know, I just know I can only find out on my own.

It's not fair for you to have to hear folks gossiping about me, I know. The island's such a wee place. You're right, there's nowhere for me to hide. I'm not sure I can try. I can't be sorry for kissing a man with a gun. Or helping a lass who might never have woken up. I'd do it again if I had to because not doing it feels like being half a person, just a wee bit of who I am. Whoever I kiss, and however embarrassed it makes you, I'll never be sorry when it doesn't feel wrong.

I suppose this letter feels funny to write because I'm not sure who's writing it. I'm kinda someone else when you're not there. I don't really know who she is, or what she'll do, because she's never been allowed out of the house. This person's not bad, I don't think, but she's not the daughter you'd want. I can't be her any more. I'm too strange. I'll always be just a kiss away from being a nice girl. Being a 'nice girl' is like being in a box. I can see so much outside of it, but I can barely move with the label wrapped around me.

I know you're scared, Ma. And you've always been fearty, right from the day your baby picked a winter butterfly off the step and placed it in her mouth. It's OK to be scared I reckon. I'm scared too, I don't know why I'm the way I am, but I can't keep apologising for it any more.

Do you remember those paper dolls you got me when I was wee? I always envied them. They came with all these outfits I could cut out and fold on. On the page, the lassie was blank, just standing there in her vest and pants, but I could dress her as a cowgirl, a magician's assistant, a teacher, a nurse. Just like that. Zap! I reckon everyone starts out as a paper doll, like we can be anyone, until people tell us we can't. That's how I feel now, like I can do anything. I can live any life I want without you insisting only one fits. Kiss the rabbit for me, kiss the canary, kiss Nan. I'm sorry I won't be able to any more. When I'm settled, I'll send a postcard to let you know I'm alive. Right now, you should know that's how I feel, a wee bit scared, but alive.

Love (it's easier to say without you butting in and doing something that gets in the way),   *Sylvie xxx*

I don't have any envelopes. I ask at the snack shop and a lady in a wool coat overhears. She's got this stack of brown envelopes and lavender notepaper. I wonder if she's writing love letters she wants to disguise as gas bills. I offer to buy the envelope off her, but she gives me two. 'Just in case.' I rip the letter out of my diary and shove it in an envelope for Ma. Then I stare at the waves. The ferry's folding the water behind us into a pathway of feathers. The gulls follow.

I don't know where I'm going when I get to the mainland. I reckon I'll hop on a bus and just stay on it until I reach somewhere worth staying put. That's the plan. As plans go it's not much, but it's mine.

LORRIE

They found the diary in the café at a station, a crescent of cola on the cover and small perfect handwriting that didn't want to be seen, yet seemed worried about being graded at the same time. Bunny came to the chemist where I'd got a job once school finished. The nights were drawing in. The church was decorated with gourds for the harvest festival. There were scarecrows everywhere, strapped to fences, propped above drystone walls for the scarecrow competition.

'I just thought I'd let you know Sylvie's not in a ditch,' Bunny said, picking up a packet of aspirin. 'Someone found her diary in Edinburgh.'

'I'm not bothered,' I said.

Sylvie had been gone for three months. The village hissed with whispers. Some said she must have had a boyfriend she ran off with. Others insisted she wasn't the sort, and Bunny probably sent her to a convent somewhere. Occasionally, I heard the odd comment I wasn't expecting. I'd hear it at work when people collected their parents' prescriptions, or came in to buy perfume for a date.

Marjorie Swift picked up a jar of hand cream and opened it. Since sewing class, her brother had joined the navy and her father had been forced to take her on as an apprentice. She was so slight she'd struggle to lift a footstool, but her hands were something else. Sturdy and long, they were strong enough to crack lobsters.

'I've been asked on a date,' she whispered. 'I don't know if I can go. He wants to go out for crabs.' She turned her hands over to show me her fingertips, so tough she wore crocheted gloves whenever she wasn't working. 'I don't think I can do that with my gloves on though. I'm sorry about your pal disappearing,' she said. 'I always liked Sylvie.'

'I never got that impression when she was here.'

'I didn't speak to her much, but when we were in the infants we sat together. There was something so calm about her. Once, I fell in the yard and she bent down and kissed it better. I never forgot that, it was so sweet.'

Marjorie left with a lotion I told her fishermen secretly buy, claiming it was for their wives. I walked home swinging my bag. Passing the church, I saw one of the posters asking for Sylvie's whereabouts. Beneath it, someone had lit a candle and placed a few flowers. *Praying you're OK, Sylvie. Come home safe.*

There were a couple of girls in kilts bumping along the lane in roller skates. They stopped at the shrine, lowered their eyes and folded their arms in the same way as their mothers.

'That poor lass. No one's seen her. I bet she's dead.'

'She might not be. I bet she fell off a cliff and hit her head and is wandering somewhere wondering who she is.'

'Yeah right! I highly doubt it.'

'It happens.'

'Where?'

'It happened in a book my Nan had.'

'I knew her, you know, she cured my sister's pet goldfish once when it had the fin rot.'

'What did she do?'

'I dunno, I wasn't there, she whispered to it or something.'

'Your sister never had a goldfish. Your ma won't have anything that dies in the place. Not even plants.'

'Well, it wasn't my sister's, it was someone she knew though. I heard that lass fixed it like Saint Francis of Assisi or something.'

The girls picked a dandelion and placed it by the candle.

'Some say she was funny, you know, crazy or something. I don't know though. What if she wasn't? And she could do stuff?'

'Like Superman and that?'

'Just like that.'

One of the girls patted the photo. 'Well, we're praying you're OK, Sylvie. Say a prayer for me, say a prayer for all our goldfish, and one for my sister too. She's got a wicked zit and is going out dancing on Saturday. Let it clear up, so she'll get married soon and I'll get my own room.'

I walked on, leaving their whispers and prayers for superheroes, giants and girls. Every so often, I'd hear something similar. Even years after I'd left the island and returned for my father's funeral to stand beside my mother and Rook, only inches apart, finally allowed to hold hands but not quite able to, a lifetime of restraint keeping them apart. I kept seeing roadside shrines dotted around the island long after the ink on the posters had faded and the paper had been lost to the wind. The schoolgirls who left dandelions and dolls at the shrines didn't know Sylvie's name. They only knew there was a girl who once lived here who could make you better. They heard she was so tall she was practically a giant. They heard she was mute. One day, she simply vanished. The facts were unclear. They only knew they had somewhere to wish their small ailments away. They had someone to understand all their prayers. It continued for so long it became part of the island, a story as whispered as the stories of selkies on the rocks and the lady in white by the lighthouse.

*

I found the diary a few days after Bunny visited the chemist. I snuck over with potato peelings, slipping our surplus rubbish into Bunny's dustbin before collection day. It was right there, covered in coffee grounds. I saw Sylvie's writing surrounded by the red and gold stripes of the Tunnock's caramel wafer wrappers she'd glued to the cover. I once asked her why she always saved them. 'I like feeling I have a sunrise in my pocket,' she'd said. 'They're a beautiful thing.'

I brushed off the cover with my dressing gown and snuck the diary inside. I could see why Bunny would want to get rid of it. It didn't contain who she saw Sylvie as. It didn't paint a pretty picture of herself. I placed the notebook on my pillow and read it. Sylvie believed she was different, her mother did too. I wondered if believing it consoled Bunny after she lost her husband, and if Sylvie would be more like everyone else if she hadn't been told there was something wrong with her. I almost felt sorry for her, until I remembered her with my father, mouth to mouth. I flicked a page and found myself at the end.

This is the last page of this diary. I might buy another. Or maybe it doesn't matter. I haven't a clue where I'm going now. Wherever it is, it won't fit here. I don't know if I'm going to be the sort of lassie who writes down her life. I reckon I'd rather be the sort of woman who's too busy living to make notes. The notebook is full. I don't need it any more. I'm done with it and the lass who wrote it. I don't fancy carrying her around wherever I go. So long.

I closed the book and got out the photo I'd kept in my drawer since the photographer had dropped off Bunny's wedding pictures and she'd slipped one into the bin. It was a blur of a girl with blood on her skirt, feathers in the air. Whoever she was, she was gone. She'd left her canary, her rabbit, and stepped out of the cage she'd built around herself. She was my friend, then she wasn't. She sometimes seemed stupid, and sometimes she was the wisest person I'd ever met. I'd often think about it and question who the girl really was. She showed me only a small part of herself – the rest was elusive as the angel's share of the spirit drifting in the air. I knew her, and I barely knew her. Honestly, that's all anyone can say about anyone.

Dear readers,

As well as relying on bookshop sales, And Other Stories relies on subscriptions from people like you for many of our books, whose stories other publishers often consider too risky to take on.

Our subscribers don't just make the books physically happen. They also help us approach booksellers, because we can demonstrate that our books already have readers and fans. And they give us the security to publish in line with our values, which are collaborative, imaginative and 'shamelessly literary'.

All of our subscribers:

- receive a first-edition copy of each of the books they subscribe to
- are thanked by name at the end of our subscriber-supported books
- receive little extras from us by way of thank you, for example: postcards created by our authors

BECOME A SUBSCRIBER, OR GIVE A SUBSCRIPTION TO A FRIEND

Visit andotherstories.org/subscriptions to help make our books happen. You can subscribe to books we're in the process of making. To purchase books we have already published, we urge you to support your local or favourite bookshop and order directly from them – the often unsung heroes of publishing.

OTHER WAYS TO GET INVOLVED

If you'd like to know about upcoming events and reading groups (our foreign-language reading groups help us choose books to publish, for example) you can:

- join our mailing list at: andotherstories.org
- follow us on Twitter: @andothertweets
- join us on Facebook: facebook.com/AndOtherStoriesBooks
- admire our books on Instagram: @andotherpics
- follow our blog: andotherstories.org/ampersand

Current & Upcoming Books

ANGELA READMAN is a twice-shortlisted winner of the Costa Short Story Award. Her debut story collection *Don't Try This at Home* was published by And Other Stories in 2015. It won The Rubery Book Prize and was shortlisted in the Edge Hill Short Story Prize. She also writes poetry, and her collection *The Book of Tides* was published by Nine Arches in 2016. *Something Like Breathing* is her first novel.